The Wainwright's Unwelcome Christmas Bride

Cheryl Wright

Copyright

THE WAINWRIGHT'S UNWELCOME CHRISTMAS BRIDE
(Unwelcome Brides Series – Book Three)

Copyright ©2024 by Cheryl Wright

Small Town Romance Publications

Dedication

To Margaret Tanner, my very dear friend and fellow author, for her enduring encouragement and friendship.

To Alan, my husband of almost fifty years, who has been a relentless supporter of my writing and dreams for many years.

To You, my wonderful readers, who encourage me to continue writing these stories. It is such a joy knowing so many of you enjoy reading my stories as much as I love writing them for you.

Table of Contents

Chapter One

She couldn't breathe. She was gagged but not bound, and savagely shoved into goodness knew what.

Whatever it was, she knew it was icy cold. Close to Christmas, it was snow weather – depending on where she happened to be. She shivered at the thought of what awaited her. If someone didn't find her, it would mean certain death.

It was dark and damp where she lay, and very uncomfortable. She tried to remember what caused her to be in this situation. Try as she might, her mind had closed down on her. One thing she did recall was being lifted by a man. That was her last memory of freedom.

The next thing she knew, she was here. Wherever *here* happened to be.

Without warning, she was jolted sideways. Thrown hard against…what? Her body stinging from the hit she had just taken.

Wriggling about, trying to lift her hands to her mouth, she finally achieved her goal of pulling the gag out of her mouth. At least she could breathe. Or so she thought. Wherever she was, there was little oxygen. And that bothered her.

She wriggled first her hands, and then her feet. At least everything seemed to be working. Except she could barely move. Her heart pounded. Where was she? She was hyperventilating. She had to slow her breathing. Conserve whatever oxygen she had left.

She called out. Softly at first, because her mouth felt dry. Incredibly dry. When she tried to shout, her voice broke and was barely audible, even to her own ears. It was an impossible task, but she was determined to get out of this alive.

After what seemed forever, she heard a high pitched sound. She had no idea what it was, but it seemed to be close by.

She was jolted again. Her pale skin must be covered in bruises, she was certain. Except it was the least of her worries. Unless someone rescued her from this airless place, she was doomed. As she tried to reserve her oxygen, she drifted into a deep sleep.

Likely never to wake again.

The woman awoke with a start. Her head hurt, along with the rest of her. She lurched forward yet again. She wished it would stop. She felt warmth on her face, and knew immediately what it was.

Blood. It was the last thing she needed.

Not that she expected to get out of this alive. She didn't. For the life of her, she couldn't fathom why someone, anyone, would do this to her. Leave her to die.

She called out when she was jolted around this time. "No!" she called out, her voice still not cooperating. "Not again!" It was futile, she knew it was, but at least it felt as though she was doing something to help herself.

The sudden silence confused her, and she waited with baited breath. Was she to be released, or transported elsewhere, never to be seen again?

She closed her eyes against the thoughts that ran through her otherwise blank mind. As she listened, muffled sounds surrounded her. She had no idea what they were.

She tried to alert them to her presence, but she was weak and could barely move. She was resigned to the fact she would die in this space she had been confined in. There was no way around it. Suddenly she was lifted and again slammed against whatever surrounded her. She was more confused than ever. How could someone lift her, but she couldn't feel them, and they couldn't see her?

Muffled voices again, then nothing. It wasn't long before she was moving again. Where to? She had no idea. If it meant freedom, then so be it. Otherwise, she would die. Her oxygen was running out, she was convinced of it.

Chapter Two

Hopetoun – 1880's

Darryl Franklin was already waiting on the platform ready for his delivery before the train arrived. He hated being late, but more than that, he wanted to ensure his order was treated with care. It wasn't that the railway workers were trying to destroy his livelihood, they simply had limited time, and instead of taking care of the goods on the train, they threw them about.

His workhorse of a wagon was already placed where they could hand everything out for Darryl to place it carefully. He sighed. Even with the promise of a big tip, he already knew there would be some damage. It happened every time.

What the town needed was a timber mill. Somewhere he could buy direct and know the timber he bought wouldn't be damaged. Sitting on the back of the wagon while he waited, Darryl dreamed of the day it would happen.

Except he knew it never would. Hopetoun was far too isolated for that. And yet, despite that, his wainwright business was thriving. He was a craftsman. Every wagon was created with care, which is why his wagons were in high demand.

The sound of the train whistle startled him back to reality. So much, he almost tumbled from the wagon.

As the train came to a halt, he moved the wagon closer still, closing the gap between the two. The door to the goods area opened, and a familiar face grinned at him. "Ready, are we, Darryl?" John Mitchell, his old school friend asked, his voice full of mirth.

The pair spent the next fifteen minutes transferring Darryl's purchases from the train to the wagon. Last to be removed was a wooden box. If the sides hadn't been straight, Darryl would have thought it a coffin. "That's not mine," he said, pointing to the offending item.

John glanced down at the paperwork he held. "It says everything in this carriage is yours. Everything else has already been offloaded at other stations."

Darryl wasn't convinced, but who was he to argue. Perhaps the supplier had sent him a gift? If he was being gifted something, Darryl hoped it was at least worthwhile. His eyes glanced over the box again. Even if the gift was near useless, he could reuse the timber it was made from. "Thank you, John," he said, shaking the other man's hand, then slipping him a greenback. "It was good to see you again."

After securing his load, Darryl headed to his workshop. In reality, his workshop was an oversized barn. His home was on the same property, a decent distance away. He was situated not far out of town – it helped to keep the noise level down in town. Besides, it gave him the peace and quiet he craved. Darryl was not one for socializing. He didn't desire human contact like other people did. He longed to be alone with his own thoughts and his own company while he worked.

Despite the snow being ploughed to the side of the road, the trip was slower than usual. He had a heavy load, and didn't want to push his horses to go faster. Another day or so and it would be impassable. With Christmas not far away, he knew the weather would become far worse. Darryl would need to secure supplies before the mercantile closed for Christmas day.

Any other time he would have done that while he was already in town. Avoiding people was his aim, but today Darryl had to get these supplies into his workshop before it snowed again. The last thing he wanted to contend with was wet timber.

Besides, there was no hurrying, since the road was slippery. He could thank the snow for that.

Darryl shrugged his shoulders. He didn't celebrate Christmas, and hadn't done so for many years. He preferred to keep to himself. It had worked so far, despite the efforts of the townsfolk to include him in their festivities.

Breathing a sigh of relief as he arrived at his property, Darryl urged the horses forward and into the large workshop. He worked alone, which meant he would unload the new supplies himself. Despite being used to doing so, he cringed at the thought. It wasn't an easy job for one man. Still, it was necessary, and he had orders to fulfil. Perhaps he could make himself a coffee first?

Shrugging his shoulders, Darryl decided against it. His workshop was chilly this time of year. Better to get it over and done with, then he could get inside his cottage and warm up. This was the hardest part of this job. More than once, Darryl had thought about hiring an assistant, but didn't know anyone who would suit the position. He shrugged his shoulders again.

He needed to bite the bullet and start unloading. As he glanced at the contents on the wagon, he wondered what the gift was the owner of the timber mill had sent him. He would check it out once he finished unloading.

~*~

With every piece of timber now where it belonged, it was time to check what was in the box. Darryl's heart rate increased in anticipation. In all the years he'd been ordering from this particular timber yard, they'd not once sent him a gift. Perhaps there were new owners. Were they now rewarding their valued customers?

The lid was nailed shut, but not properly. There was a small gap. Darryl was convinced he could open it using only his hands, and it did move slightly, but not enough. He reached for a hammer.

His back turned, Darryl heard something. At least he thought he did. It was gone now. Maybe it was the wind whistling through the workshop? This weather brought all sorts of strange sounds.

Turning back, he focused on opening the box and finding the treasure he'd been gifted. It was heavy, and had taken both Darryl and John to place it on the wagon. He struggled to unload it alone.

Darryl moved around the box as he loosened the nails, until finally, he was able to remove the lid. He stared down in disbelief. Had he known the contents, he would have removed the lid first. His heart pounded, and his mind was in confusion. Why would anyone send him a box with a dead woman in it?

Admonishing himself for not the first time, Darryl stared at the woman laying dead in his workshop.

There was blood in her hair. And on her face and hands. How long had she been there in the box? He was certain she would have died from lack of oxygen. Although the blood seemed to say otherwise.

No matter what happened to her, he needed to drive back into town and fetch the sheriff. He shook his head in disbelief. Why was she sent to *him*? It was baffling. Darryl didn't know the woman, had never set eyes on her before. Perhaps it was random? The more he thought about it, the more confused he became.

He began to walk away. Should he reseal the box, to preserve the body, or leave it open? Critters had no way of entering his workshop, so leaving it open should be fine. Except it seemed callous to leave the unfortunate woman laying there like that. His heart pounding, Darryl turned back to reseal the box, or perhaps sit the lid on it. In his panicked state, he stumbled.

Suddenly the woman sat upright, her hands outstretched. Darryl ran to her side, swearing under his breath for not checking her pulse. Not knowing she was alive. Almost the moment he was by her side, the woman collapsed back into the box. Luckily he was there to stop her head hitting the hard timber that had already maimed her.

Chapter Three

She wasn't sure how she managed to sit up, but it took all her strength and determination to do so. The sudden surge of oxygen had literally brought her back from the brink of death.

Glancing about, she didn't know where she was. It had the distinct smell of freshly cut timber, she knew that much. As she gazed about, she noticed a man. Was he the one who did this to her? He didn't seem familiar but that meant nothing. Her mind was one of confusion and concern.

His back to her, she wasn't sure what to do. She was weak. Far too weak to escape. Suddenly he turned and strode toward her, muttering something under his breath. It was all too much, and everything went black.

When she awoke, she was cradled in the stranger's arms. He carried her outside, then into a nearby cottage. It was warm and cozy. He said nothing, but placed her on the sofa and covered her in a blanket.

He didn't say a word, but walked over to the fire. The stranger's back was now to her. He was stoking and feeding the fire. She was grateful for the warmth, but was she safe? Between the heat of the fire and the thickness of the blanket, she was comfortable. Unlike when she was sealed in that timber box.

She swallowed, hard. Tears sprung to her eyes, but she refused to let them fall.

As she stared at his back, she couldn't help but wonder – was this the man who abducted her? If it was, why was he now helping her? She was convinced he wasn't her kidnapper. She didn't feel afraid of him, not even a little bit. There was a peacefulness about him. His presence calmed her. After all she'd been through, it was clear she could trust this man.

She continued to study him, not wanting to take her eyes off him. She needed to know he wouldn't harm her, but wasn't certain how to do that.

He stood, then turned to face her. "I'll make you a cup of tea," he said gently. "Then I'll take a look at your injuries."

"Thank you," she said. Or at least tried to say. The dryness of her mouth stopped the words from forming.

He nodded gently, then left the room. He was gone for a few minutes before returning. Placing a mug of tea on a side table, he helped her to sit up.

Handing her the tea, he stayed close by. His big strong hands suddenly covered her small shaking hands. He said nothing, but helped her to drink.

The warmth of the tea as it slid down her throat was…restorative. Soothing. She had never enjoyed tea so much as she did right now. "Thank you," she said this time, the words quiet but audible.

"Of course," he said gently. "I'm Darryl Franklin, and this is my home. Do you know what happened? Why you were in that box?" He was frowning, but angry at the same time. Not angry at her, she was certain, but at whomever put her in that box.

She shook her head slightly. "I have no idea. My mind is foggy," she said softly.

"What is your name?" His voice was gentle but commanding, but it was already clear he was trustworthy.

She closed her eyes and tried to think. "I…I don't know," she finally said. "All I remember is someone carrying me. After that, I can't recall much at all. Until you rescued me," she said, her tears now unleashed.

He stared into her eyes. She saw the pity on his face. It was hard to miss. Moments later, he pulled a handkerchief from his pocket, and wiped at her tears. Then he handed it to her. "I'll have to let the sheriff know what happened," he said gently. "But not until you feel up to it." She nodded, then took another sip. "I'll check out your injuries, too," he said, then began to walk away.

Reaching out, she grabbed his hand. "Don't leave me. Please," she begged. Since when was she afraid to be alone? Since some crazed person had tried to kill her, that's when. Her heart pounded, and she felt light headed. It was the stress, she knew it was. She'd been through so much over the past days. Time had been a black hole. How long had she been locked in that box?

"Do you feel up to seeing the sheriff today?" he asked quietly.

How should she answer? Should she say no and hope Darryl Franklin accepted it? Or should she go with him to visit the sheriff's office? Her heart pounded. No matter what she did or didn't do, it didn't change a thing.

Someone had tried to murder her. She may never know why.

~*~

Sitting across from the sheriff was nerve wracking. She knew it had to happen, sometime, but wasn't ready. The problem was the weather. According to Darryl, they couldn't wait. There would be heavier snow tomorrow, he told her. That meant the road would be snowbound, and they wouldn't get through.

Darryl said he didn't like the thought of keeping her at his home without medical treatment, or knowing she was safe. It made her wonder – safe from who? Her mind was still foggy, and she didn't understand the reason.

Perhaps he had a point?

"What is your name?" Sheriff Peter Dodd asked gently. "And where are you from?" He leaned toward the pair sitting on the other side, pen in hand. When she didn't answer, he studied her.

"I should have taken her to the doc first," Darryl said. "She has a head injury." The sheriff stared then, trying to see the injury. "I cleaned it up as best I could," he added.

Without warning, the sheriff sat upright, then scribbled something on his notepad. "Let's go then," he said, indicating the door. "We'll go together. I need more information before I can do anything."

The woman was more confused than ever. Why was the sheriff leaving with them? And where were they going? Her head was spinning, but no information was forthcoming. She glanced up at Darryl, hoping he could help. His expression proved he was as confused as she was.

"Why are you coming to the Doc's?" Darryl demanded, his expression one of annoyance.

"To find out the truth." The sheriff hurried to get ahead of them, and held the door open for them to enter. "Mornin' Doc," he said as the pair entered the doctor's rooms. "This here lady needs your attention."

The sheriff was talking as though she wasn't there. It made her feel helpless as the doctor glanced from one to the other of the men. "What's the problem? Why are you here, Sheriff?" They began to talk at the same time, making it impossible to understand either man. "Darryl, you tell me."

Her heart pounded as her rescuer explained what had occurred. The doctor nodded his head, then turned to her. "My dear," he said gently, "you go into the examination room and sit down. I'll be with you in a moment."

He closed the door and stepped toward her. She flinched. She had no idea why – it was an automatic reaction.

"What happened to you?" the kindly doctor asked. "Do you even know?" He put his hands to her shoulder, and she recoiled. "I'm going to check your head," he said gently. "We'll get to the bottom of it, don't you worry."

She truly hoped he was right. Because at this point, she had no idea who she was, where she was from, or why she was sent here in a wooden box. What she did know was someone had made her afraid. Very afraid. It was not a pleasant situation to be in.

Doc Spencer helped her onto the examination table, then gave her a good going over. It was surprising the number of injuries he found. Her arms were badly bruised, which was no surprise. Nor was she surprised her head needed stitches. He cleaned up the remaining blood on her face, then sat her down to talk.

The doc reached out and held her hand. "Do you have any memory of what happened?" he asked, but she didn't. Shaking her head hurt, and she did so gently. "You appear to have amnesia," he told her. "There is no treatment, except for rest." He stood, and helped her to her feet, then took her out to the waiting room.

"I've stitched her head, but the remainder of the injuries are superficial. The bruises will change color over the next few days. Best thing is for the patient to rest." His eyes went from the sheriff to Darryl. They seemed to be questioning.

At first, she wasn't sure what he was asking. Her mind was still foggy, but she finally understood. "I...I don't have any money," she whispered. "Perhaps I can withdraw some from the bank?"

Both men looked at her blankly. It was then she understood. "I have no memory of who I am. My reticule is missing, which means I have no proof either."

The sheriff nodded, and the severity of her situation finally sunk in. As someone who had no memory of who she was, or any proof of identity, she was destitute. No money, no clothes, and no memory. It was not a good position to be in. Her heart pounded. What would she do now?

"I have a spare room," Darryl said, but the sheriff grunted. "It's only temporary," he said firmly.

"I can't allow an unaccompanied woman to stay with you." The sheriff's words were firm.

Darryl spun around to face him. "It is not your choice. It is up to…" he paused, and she knew it was because he didn't know her name. "this unfortunate woman, not you," he said. His words were far more commanding than the sheriff's. Did he believe he was responsible for her, since he was her rescuer?

"It is not up to either of you," Doc Spencer said. "It's up to *my* patient. The other option is the boarding house. She would be well looked after there."

"Except I have no money," she whispered.

Sheriff Dodd was stoney faced through all of this, but his expression suddenly changed. "I have an allowance for these situations," he offered. "The town will cover the cost."

She felt overwhelmed, and emotional. "Thank you, Sheriff Dodd. I appreciate that."

The sheriff opened the door and indicated for her to go ahead. She complied. Darryl followed them. Did he not trust the sheriff, or was it something else entirely? No matter, she was happy to know she would be safe and well fed at the boarding house.

Chapter Four

Darryl was fuming. How dare Sheriff Dodd make insinuations about his offer for the woman to stay with him. He was a law abiding citizen, and would never intentionally put a woman's reputation at risk.

As the three of them walked toward the boarding house, his anger became more annoyance. Why he was feeling so protective, he didn't know. Perhaps it was because he'd found and rescued the stranger.

No matter the reason, the sheriff had no right to tell anyone what to do unless they were breaking the law. The three stopped when they reached the boarding house. The woman glanced at the small garden out front, then staring at the roofline, checked the building out. There were pretty curtains on each window, and that no doubt appealed to her.

The front door opened, and the owner stepped forward. A frown on her face, she addressed the newcomers. "Good morning, Sheriff Dodd, Darryl." She stared at the woman momentarily, then reached out a hand. "I'm Maggie Goldsmith. What's your name Hun?"

Maggie wasn't to know, and the woman appeared confused. Darryl wasn't surprised – she was in a difficult situation. "I…I don't know," she answered, sounding even more confused than earlier.

After staring at her blankly for a few short seconds, Maggie moved closer and pulled her into a hug. "Oh you poor thing," she whispered loud enough the men heard. "You come inside, I'll look after you." Maggie led the woman inside, and the two men stared at each other.

"What just happened?" Darryl asked, not sure he'd get an answer.

"Maggie being Maggie. Give her a minute." Sheriff Dodd scratched his head, then pushed his hair back into place. It wasn't long and the door opened again.

"No luggage?" Maggie asked the moment she was outside again. "What is she supposed to do for clothes?" She seemed genuinely concerned. Neither man knew, but Maggie didn't give them time to answer any questions. "That woman who ran off after you questioned her, Sheriff, she left her belongings behind. They might fit." With that, she turned around, went inside, and closed the door.

She didn't even give the sheriff a chance to make arrangements for payment. That told Darryl a lot. Maggie Goldsmith was a decent person who would look after the stranger. Darryl wasn't sure why, but he felt relieved at the knowledge she would be well cared for.

Now all they needed to do was discover her identity, and find out what had happened to her.

~*~

Darryl decided to get supplies while he was in town. It wasn't that he had far to go to get them, it was more finding time. This close to Christmas, he was always busy. Either his customers needed their wagons repaired, or they placed orders for new wagons. Hence the reason he had such a large order for timber this time.

That thought made him ponder. How did the box with the woman inside it get into his order? Did that mean someone at the timber yard was culpable? Or was the perpetrator simply at the right place at the perfect time?

It could be either, and he may never know the answer. Darryl wished he could do more to help the woman, but had no idea how he could accomplish it. At least now he knew she was safe and would be well looked after with Maggie.

Darryl glanced down at the empty cardboard box he held, and shivered. His mind was everywhere except where it needed to be, and that was on getting supplies. He reached for a bag of sugar and placed it in the box. He needed coffee, that was a given, sausages, eggs, and baked beans. Potatoes would be handy too. His mind wasn't cooperating – there was something else he needed, but he couldn't think what that might be.

At the front counter, he finally remembered – butter and milk. The amount he'd bought probably wouldn't be enough to see him through to Christmas, but he could easily return. Today had been traumatic, not only for him, but especially for the unknown woman. His heart thudded merely thinking of her. He couldn't imagine how confused she must be. She was in a place she didn't know, amongst complete strangers. Not knowing who she was would have to be playing on her mind.

 Darryl reached for his wallet when he spotted them. The sight caught him off guard. "I'll take a bunch of mixed flowers too, thanks," he told the mercantile owner. Surely flowers would cheer the woman up? Even if it was only a little, it would be worth the effort.

Darryl pulled out his wallet and paid in cash. He didn't like to owe money. He ran his business with cash. Accounts meant he waited for up to a month for payment, and he didn't like that. Particularly when it was such a large amount.

After placing the box of groceries on the buggy, he strolled down to the boarding house. Maggie opened the door when he knocked, and smiled when she saw what he held in his hands. "She'll love those," Maggie said, then ushered him inside.

He frowned. "I don't want to make a fuss," he said. "I thought they might cheer her up."

Maggie quirked an eyebrow. "I'm sure they will," she said. "I feel so bad for her, but she'll be fine here. I promise to take good care of her."

Warmth filled him. Darryl wasn't sure why, but wondered if it was because he knew the woman was now in good hands. "On second thought," he said as he stood in the sitting room, "you can give them to her." His arms outstretched, Darryl tried to hand the bouquet of flowers over, but Maggie was having none of it.

"It's your gift, you need to deliver it," she said firmly, then disappeared from the room. In every other way, Darryl was a confident man. When it came to dealing with people, particularly women, he was the complete opposite. He stood where Maggie left him, feeling more than a little awkward. Why, he had no idea. It wasn't like he was taking her on a date. It was simply an act of kindness on his part.

The woman he'd rescued entered the room, her eyes glancing briefly at the flowers. She quickly moved her gaze to his face. "I thought you'd be gone by now," she said quietly.

He reached out and handed her the flowers. "These are for you," he said. She seemed reluctant to take them. "I saw them at the mercantile when I was refilling my supplies. I hoped they would brighten your day." Brighten her day? Darryl wanted to slap himself – what a stupid thing to say, given the circumstances.

Moments before he pulled his eyes away, Darryl noticed the slow smile that came to her lips. It made him smile, too. She had little to smile about, so he was glad he'd made the effort.

"Thank you," she said, her voice quiet. She sniffed the fragrance and glanced up at him again. "I appreciate it."

His heart hammered. What did that mean? It had nothing to do with the woman. He'd only met her a short time ago. It had him confused. "I should go," he said, already moving toward the door. "I…have an order to fulfill." It wasn't a lie, but he could have lingered. Except spending time with her was not a good thing.

These feelings he was having, they were not something he wanted. He shook himself mentally. He felt sorry for her, that was all. Since he was the one who found her, there was an attachment of sorts. That was all it was. He was convinced of it, and would ensure he remembered it.

She nodded, and sniffed the flowers again. "Well, thank you, again." She said the words so softly, he almost missed them.

He hurried to the door as Maggie reentered the room. "You must stay for lunch," she said before he had a chance to get out of the door and onto the street where he could breathe again.

"I, ah…" He muttered, trying to refuse the invitation the best way he could without appearing rude. "I have milk and butter on my buggy. I can't leave them there." It was the best he could think of on the spur of the moment.

Maggie put her hands to her hips, and the look she gave him was almost frightening. "It is snowing. The weather is colder than an icebox." She continued to scowl. "Please stay," she said.

Darryl felt like he had no choice, and reneged. "Thank you for your kindness," he said. "I wasn't thinking straight. Of course I will stay for lunch."

"Wonderful," Maggie said, rubbing her hands together. "Come through to the kitchen. It's only the three of us for lunch. We don't need to be formal, do we?"

"Indeed we don't," he said, wondering what he'd got himself into.

Chapter Five

Why did Darryl bring her flowers? She sniffed them again and breathed in the enticing aroma. Darryl said it was to brighten her day. It had been a heck of a day, that was for sure. But now she was confused.

It was usual for men courting a woman to present her with flowers. But not when the woman was a complete stranger, as she was. They certainly weren't courting.

She stopped herself from shrugging, as it would be rude to do so.

"Take a seat, Darryl," Maggie said.

He looked stunned. As though he had no idea what was going on. It was exactly how she felt. Perhaps if the sheriff was able to determine her identity, things would be different. As it was right now, she didn't even know her name. Maggie had taken to calling her *Hun*, and what was worse, she was responding to it.

Still, Maggie meant well. There wasn't an evil bone in her body. The woman was so kind and caring.

Maggie had even supplied her with clothes left behind by a previous boarder.

"How are you settling in?" Darryl asked.

She'd not been here even an hour, so his question was surprising. "Fine," she said. "Maggie is treating me well." She turned and smiled at Maggie, and was rewarded with a returning smile. It made her feel warm inside. And wanted.

Definitely wanted.

Maggie placed a bowl of thick vegetable soup in front of her, and also Darryl. "Thank you," she said quietly. She wasn't sure why, but her voice was hoarse. Perhaps from the lack of oxygen?

After placing another bowl where she would sit, Maggie added sliced bread in the center of the table. "It's not long out of the oven, so still warm," she told them, then pushed the butter toward Darryl. He in turn pushed it to her.

The man had manners. That was beyond doubt a redeeming trait. So far she'd found nothing to show he was less than he seemed. "Do you need help?" Darryl asked gently. Was that because she sat at the table waiting for everyone else to start eating?

Instead of answering, she sat there, not moving. She wasn't sure why. He reached for a slice of the warm bread and buttered it. Surprisingly, once it was ready, he slid it over to her, and took her empty bread plate.

Was she losing her mind? She couldn't even butter a slice of bread for herself. Maggie had ensured she ate when she arrived, saying she must be malnourished. Perhaps Maggie was right. She couldn't think straight. She couldn't have been in that box very long. Could she? Wouldn't she have died from lack of oxygen?

"The lid wasn't on tight," Darryl said gently. Despite his quiet words, she was startled. Had she said the words out loud? "It's probably what saved you." He reached across and covered her hand with his.

A shiver went through her. She quickly pulled her hand away. Darryl moved his hand away from her, and reached for another slice of bread. Maggie sat quietly, watching their interactions. She seemed happy about what she saw.

Shaking her head, her gaze sat on Darryl. "I don't understand why someone did this to me. Does that mean I'm a bad person?" she asked, her voice breaking as she spoke.

"Not at all," Maggie said. "It means whoever did this to you is wicked."

"I agree," Darryl said. "Pure evil. A normal person wouldn't do something like that." His face was filled with compassion, and it endeared him to her even further.

Maggie glanced from one to the other of them. "Eat up while your food is hot. There's plenty of time for talk afterwards." Maggie was right. She picked up her spoon and took a mouthful of the thick soup. It tasted as delicious as it smelled. Darryl seemed to be enjoying it too.

"Coffee, Darryl?" Maggie asked when they finished eating. Without waiting for an answer, she stood and cleared the table. Darryl had two bowls of the soup, which seemed to please Maggie.

"Thank you, Maggie. I should be going." He began to stand, but Maggie put a hand to his shoulder.

"The meal isn't over yet. I know how hard you work," she said. "Give yourself a break. You deserve it."

He nodded, and resumed his place at the table. "You're a good soul, Maggie," he said. "I appreciate it."

With that, Maggie took the soiled dishes to the sink, then pulled a pie from the oven. "Freshly baked apple pie. I know you'll have some Darryl. If you're like most men, you don't cook for yourself."

She watched the interaction between the two, and decided Maggie and Darryl were known to each other. Did that mean Maggie had fed him in the past? She wouldn't put it past the other woman. Maggie seemed the nurturing type.

It made her think about herself. Was she the nurturing type? What did she do for a living? Was she married? She immediately glanced down at her hands. No rings, so the assumption was she was single. That had to be a good thing, didn't it? No husband meant no one to worry about her. Except there could be siblings, or even parents. She was in an impossible situation, with no way out.

Suddenly, tears sprang to her eyes. They ran down her cheeks, and she swiped at them. "I'm destitute." It was a statement, not a question. Until someone worked out her identity, there was nothing she could do to help herself.

Everyone in town had been wonderful. They were all friendly and looked after her. She only hoped she didn't have a tarnished past she wanted to keep hidden. Was she a…soiled dove? The mere thought had her reviling herself. Surely she would know if her life had been so awful? She closed her eyes and swiped at the hot tears rolling down her face.

She felt arms come around her. "Everything will turn out alright, Hun. You wait and see," Maggie said, as she hugged her tight. She was right. Maggie was a good woman, and if she stayed here long enough, they might become good friends.

Chapter Six

As much as he enjoyed the meal, and the company, Darryl knew he should head back home. He had an order to complete, although he'd be the first to admit it wasn't urgent. The due date for this wagon wasn't until mid-January.

He could afford to linger a little longer. He was, after all, enjoying himself. The only drawback was he felt awful for *Hun*. The woman was more than a little bewildered. It wasn't surprising. He'd watched as she studied her hands, her ring finger in particular. It was painfully obvious she was trying to figure out who she was. Darryl couldn't blame her.

The not knowing was the worst part. At least if it happened to someone in town, the other townsfolk would be able to advise the victim. For *Hun*, it was not possible. It had to be eating her up. "Maggie, the meal was magnificent," Darryl said as though nothing was bothering him. "And the company even better." He grinned, and Maggie smiled. *Hun* did the same. It wasn't like she had a lot to smile about, except she was alive.

Darryl pondered the thought if he hadn't opened the box when he did, she might be dead. Thankfully it wasn't tightly sealed. Likely an oversight on the would-be murderer's part. He wondered if there was a way to find out where the box was loaded on the train. Except he already knew there wasn't. It wasn't listed on the inventory, according to his friend John Mitchell. If anyone would know, it was him.

"Shall we move to the sitting room where it's more comfortable?" Maggie asked. Darryl knew there was no point arguing. Maggie always got her way. She ushered both her guests ahead of her, then disappeared back into the kitchen.

When she appeared again, Maggie had fresh drinks for them all. He was being spoiled, but Darryl knew he was not the target for her kindness. This was all about her mysterious guest. It made him wonder how long it would take for her memory to return, if it ever did. He'd heard of such things before. In one case, it had taken almost a year for the person's memory to resurface. He hoped that was not the case this time.

"Maggie was kind enough to supply me with clothes," Hun said. Perhaps not enjoying the silence? "They fit perfectly," she added.

"It was nothing." Maggie reiterated her earlier comments. "They belonged to a woman who skipped town. Sheriff Dodd had interviewed her about items stolen from the mercantile. She disappeared after that. It was months ago. I doubt we'll ever see her again."

Hun studied her momentarily. "Well, I appreciate it," she said firmly. "It means a lot to me. If only someone could hand my memory to me, I'd be very happy." She glanced down at her hands in her lap, and Darryl felt a tug at his heart. What she'd endured, and where she was now, without her memory or her belongings must be awful. He couldn't begin to imagine how she felt.

If she were in a large town or city, she'd likely be in an asylum by now. The thought tugged at his heart. Again.

Darryl drank down his remaining coffee, and stood. "I really must go. Thank you, Maggie, for the invitation, and the magnificent meal. It is always appreciated."

He glanced across at Hun. She seemed disappointed he was leaving, but Darryl couldn't fathom why. Unless she believed he held the key to who she was. Except that was far from the truth - he had no clue. Darryl wished he did.

~*~

As he sanded the wagon he was making, Darryl thought about the events of the morning. It was bad enough he had found the woman in the box. Especially the fact she was alive. Who would do such a heinous thing? He felt saddened about the situation, but knew he would feel far worse had he found her deceased.

Darryl shook himself mentally. Sanding timber was always therapeutic for him, but not today. He worried over *Hun*. She was completely alone in the world. What if her identity was never discovered? What would she do then?

Sheriff Dodd promised to look into it, to find out who she was. He was also determined to find out where she came from and how she had ended up in that dreaded box. Darryl's heart thudded at the thought of her never knowing who she was. He'd seen for himself she struggled with not knowing. Darryl appreciated how truly difficult that must be for her.

He swore under his breath as the sand paper tore under his grip. Darryl ended up with wood splinters in his fingers. It was nothing new, and was his own fault. His mind was working overtime, thinking about the stranger.

Glancing across the workshop, his eyes trained in on the wooden box sitting next to the timber he'd purchased. It was an unassuming box, and there was no need for him to even begin to imagine a woman lay dying inside it.

Darryl shook himself mentally. He might as well have stayed in town, as Maggie wanted. It was far too late now. The two women would be settling in for their nightly meal. He wondered what they might be having. Maggie was an excellent cook, and the mere thought of it made his mouth water.

Instead of giving in to his wishes, Darryl found a fresh piece of sand paper, and began sanding again. The moment he finished, he would go home and begin making his meal of sausages and eggs.

Chapter Seven

Sitting in her bedroom, Hun stared out the window. Dusk had arrived, and it was beginning to darken outside. She watched the sunset on the horizon, and pondered.

Hun wondered about who she was. For the moment she would have to be content with being Hun. More importantly, she hoped she was a good person. Everyone she'd met here so far had been decent law-abiding people. They all looked out for her, and ensured she was safe and well looked after. All that despite her not having money to repay them.

If only there was some way for her to find out. Doc Spencer said her memory may come back in days, or it could be months. There was also a possibility it would never come back. Especially given she'd been deprived of oxygen. She wasn't certain she could cope with that. Although there was no choice.

She turned at the tap on her door. "Supper is ready, Hun," Maggie called. It was a blessed interruption. Her mind was going to all sorts of places she didn't want it to go. The unknown bothered her the most.

Having no name was difficult, but worrying about her past worried her even more.

"Coming," she said, then stood. She could sit at the window for hours watching the sun go down, but knew it wasn't good for her. Maggie said she was worried, but what could either of them do about it? She was certain there was nothing anyone could do for her until she remembered who she was.

Maggie was still there when she opened the door. Dear Maggie, her new friend. "How are you feeling, Hun?" Maggie asked before looping their arms. They wandered to the kitchen in a leisurely fashion. There seemed to be no hurry, which suited her fine.

"What do you think of Darryl?" Maggie asked gently.

Did Maggie really expect her to answer? She barely knew the man. He'd saved her life then brought her to town. Apart from having lunch with them, that was the extent of her knowledge. "He seems alright, I guess," Hun said. "He did save my life."

"Yes, he did," Maggie told her. "Darryl is a hardworking man. He will do anything for anyone who needs his help. Sadly, he spends most of his time in his workshop."

"His workshop?" She closed her eyes and her mind went back to when she was rescued. Darryl had removed the lid. He'd saved her. There was no doubt in her mind. How he'd obtained that makeshift *coffin* was beyond her, but the fact remained, what he did saved her life.

She pictured the workshop now. There were long pieces of timber everywhere she looked. "I remember his workshop now," she said, and Maggie smiled.

"Good. It's time to eat," Maggie told her, and began to dish out their meal.

~*~

Maggie washed the dishes, and she dried. Maggie insisted she could do it alone, but *Hun* needed a distraction. This was it.

"What will you do if your memory doesn't come back?" Maggie asked.

Hun pondered the question. "I don't want to think about the possibility." She dried the frying pan far longer than was necessary. "There has to be a way to find out my identity," she added. She bent down to put the frying pan back where it belonged.

Studying her, Maggie scowled. "Don't think that way, Hun. It will all turn out in the end. You'll see."

Except Hun wasn't sure that was the case. With no proof of identity, she could be stuck here with no name and no knowledge of her former life. It could take years to find out who she was. If only someone knew where she'd been loaded onto the train. Surely one of the workers must remember? Although she had to acknowledge there were dozens of train stations where it could have happened.

"Someone has to know who I am," she whispered, trying to fight back the tears that threatened to fall. "Can't the sheriff find out?"

Shaking her head, Maggie dried her hands and wrapped her arms around her new boarder. "Sheriff Dodd is a good man, and an excellent sheriff," she said quietly. "If there is information to be found, I can guarantee he will find it." She tightened her grip and held Hun close. The small gesture made Hun feel far better. Maggie cared, and that was important. Everyone she'd met here in town so far had helped her in some way. What Darryl did for her was the most significant of all. He had literally saved her life. She would never forget it.

When the dishes were done and the kitchen back in order, they retired to the sitting room. As much as the kitchen was cozy and warm, the sitting room made Hun feel more at ease. With a roaring fire, and comfortable chairs, it gave her a sense of home.

"Are you alright, Hun?" Maggie asked, concern on her face.

Did that mean she appeared unhappy? Right now, she felt comfortable and happy. "I'm fine," she said honestly. "Sitting here, with you, in this wonderful room, I feel…happy. I know it sounds strange, but it feels like home." All that despite not knowing where home was, or what it looked like.

"Oh, Hun, you poor thing. That must be difficult for you. I can't even imagine.." Maggie began.

Hun shook her head. "It's alright, I promise. I have decided to live in the here and now. If the sheriff finds out who I am, and where I'm from, I'll be happy too. But for now, here with you, I feel wanted and joyful."

Maggie reached across and took her hand, then squeezed it. "I am certain Peter, er, Sheriff Dodd will find the truth. He's good at that. In the meantime, you are welcome to stay here with me." She smiled, and Hun felt comforted. She leaned back in the chair and allowed the warmth of the fire wash over her. She felt as though she was being cleansed. From what, she was uncertain, and again that thought of soiled doves crept into her mind. If she was a soiled dove, she needed to change her life. Perhaps this was an opportunity of sorts. One that would allow her to start over. Except she didn't know what she could do instead.

Did she have any qualifications? She could perhaps become a teacher. Or work in the mercantile. Her mind went back to the stores they passed on their way to the boarding house. She was still too stunned to have taken much notice.

In a day or so, she might feel up to taking a stroll around town. The fresh air would surely do her good.

Maggie squeezed her hand. "Why don't you go to bed, Hun? It won't be long and I'll do the same."

Hun turned to face her and smiled. "It's a good idea. I was beginning to doze." She stood then, and headed toward her room. She was grateful for the items the other woman had left behind. Because of her, Hun had a full wardrobe of clothes, including nightgowns. Without them, she'd be wearing the same clothes each and every day.

Never did she think her life would be reduced to this. Hun paused. Was that a glimpse into who she was? She may never know, but it was a positive sign, she felt sure.

As she glanced around the room, her eyes fell to the window. Hun was tired, but didn't want to go to sleep. What if she had nightmares? Instead, she sat in the comfortable chair by the window, and glanced out. There wasn't much to see at this hour of the night. It was dark, and most of the stores had closed by now. Still, there were some stores with light showing. It looked pretty, but not functional.

The dark sky only added to her tiredness, and Hun prepared for bed. When morning came, would she know who she was? She certainly hoped so. Not knowing the truth was taking its toll on her.

Chapter Eight

Darryl finished work on the commissioned wagon. It was too dark to do anymore now, despite the several lanterns he had set up nearby. He turned them all off except for one. He'd need that to find his way out of the large workshop, and across to his cottage.

It was a small cottage, but it was functional, and it was home. He'd lived here for many years, and never had any problems. Darryl liked living alone, despite the townsfolk trying to marry him off. Why did he need a wife when he was happy the way he was?

He shook himself mentally. Why he was worrying about what other people thought, he had no idea. His opinion was all that mattered. He pulled on his thick coat, then ventured outside into the cold. Snow covered the pathway between his workshop and cottage. Grabbing the large broom he kept for this very reason, he cleared the pathway. Then Darryl went inside and stoked the fire in the sitting room. It was still burning, but not enough to sustain the evening.

He threw some logs on the embers, and poked at it with the metal poker. Once he was satisfied, he stood. Darryl glanced around the room. It felt empty. Never before had he felt this way. The townsfolk with their constant badgering – they were responsible for him feeling like this. Darryl was certain of it.

It had absolutely nothing to do with the unknown woman he rescued. Of course it didn't. People could argue otherwise, but Darryl would not believe it.

He strolled into the kitchen, and poked at the fire in the woodstove. It was low as well. He knew better. He should have checked both before going into his workshop. His routine was all messed up. All because of that woman.

Guilt filled him at the thought. It wasn't her fault, not at all. She was an innocent victim in all of this. Her situation made him wonder. He would be interested to find out what her name was, and what her previous life was like. He truly hoped she would remember something. It must be terrible for her, losing her memory.

He shuffled about in the pantry, trying to decide what to eat. His mind went back to Hun and Maggie. What did they eat tonight? Darryl shook his head. Why did he even care? He was quite capable of cooking for himself. He didn't need a wife to do that.

All he wanted was to live his life in peace, and to have a thriving business. He already had both those things, so why was he thinking anything different?

As he pulled the frying pan out of the cupboard and let it heat up on the now hot stove, his mind wandered back to Hun and her situation. Was she still in danger? It occurred to him the person who did this might want assurance she was gone. If they found out she was alive…

He didn't want to think about it.

Darryl tried to block the thought from his mind, and threw four sausages in the frying pan. As they sizzled and cooked, the aroma was enticing. But Maggie's kitchen always smelled far more appealing. Is that what it would be like if he had a wife?

No! He wouldn't give into those types of thoughts. He was happy on his own. Had been for years. He turned the sausages, and stood staring down at them. He had to block his mind of all thoughts of Hun. He was certain she wouldn't be thinking that way.

A short time later he was eating the food he'd cooked. Normally Darryl enjoyed sausages and eggs. Tonight, not so much. The food seemed bland, and he wasn't sure why. Except he'd been spoiled with Maggie's food. That's all he could put it down to.

He'd eaten at Maggie's before. Not often, but now and then when he was in town around meal times, she had invited him to join herself and any boarders she had at the time. The moment an invitation left her lips, his senses enticed him to accept. Often Sheriff Dodd was there, too.

As far as Darryl was concerned, Maggie's cooking was far better than the food they dished up at the diner. Meals there were fancy. They probably had to be. Who wanted to go to a diner and have plain food dished up to them?

In Maggie's kitchen you were assured of good old fashioned cooking. The sort of food Darryl enjoyed. If only he could manage that sort of cooking himself.

Darryl shrugged – he had to face facts. He would never be able to prepare meals of Maggie's caliber. He doubted anyone could.

As he cleaned his kitchen from the mess he'd made, Darryl decided he was right to not want a wife. They would not meet his expectations when it came to cooking. That was on him, not the woman he might have married.

If only Maggie was a decade younger.

~*~

Tossing and turning all night was not Darryl's opinion of a good night's sleep. His sleep had been fitful at best. He lay awake staring at the ceiling for the majority of time, and had even got out of bed and went into the sitting room. He sat as close to the fire as he could get, hoping the heat would make him sleepy. When it seemed to be working, he went back to bed, to no avail.

In the end, he made a pallet close to the fire, ensuring the blankets he'd used couldn't catch fire. It was the best thing he could have done. Strangely, Darryl never had trouble sleeping. He worked hard all day, and was always ready for bed soon after supper.

Except today was not a normal day. After finding what he initially thought to be a dead woman, in his workshop no less, then to find she was alive – it was all too much. The visions of earlier today played on his mind. Darryl couldn't imagine what *Hun* was going through, if his mind was playing on him like this.

Perhaps he should visit her today. Convince himself she was alive and well. In his nightmares, she never opened her eyes. Nor did she breathe. Assuring himself she was fine would hopefully end his nightmares, and allow him to get a good night's sleep. Heaven knew he needed it.

With his decision made, Darryl closed his eyes and finally slept. When he awoke again, the sun had already risen. He quickly dressed while the kettle boiled. He would have breakfast, and work until it was a reasonable time to visit the boarding house.

Yes, that's what he would do. He had plenty of time to finish work on the commissioned wagon, so his plan would work well.

It wasn't that he *wanted* to see Hun, far from it. Darryl simply needed to reassure himself she was doing well.

Chapter Nine

With breakfast over, and the kitchen restored to its normal state of tidiness, Hun retired to the sitting room. Maggie said she was spending too much time in her room. It was true. All she did was stare out the window and fret about her situation.

Instead she stared out the window of the sitting room. She and Maggie took in the warmth of the fire as they sipped tea. "It looks like a beautiful day," Maggie said out of the blue. "You should go for a walk. Take in some of the sunshine while it's there."

Hun did a double-take. *Sunshine? In the middle of winter?* She managed to hold back a chuckle. "I imagine the sun will be gone soon. It will be replaced with snow," she said matter-of-factly, glancing at Maggie as she did so.

"Perhaps you are right," Maggie said, then drank down the last of her tea. "Christmas is almost upon us. Snow is part of the holiday season around these parts." She stood, and headed into the kitchen with both their empty mugs.

Maggie hadn't left the room long, when there was a knock at the door. Hun froze. Who would be calling at this early hour? Perhaps it was Sheriff Dodd.

"Would you mind getting that?" Maggie called from the kitchen.

Her heart pounding, Hun reluctantly opened the door. Her concern lay in the fact her would-be murderer could have located her and try again. Except, would he knock on the door?

She convinced herself he wouldn't, and opened the door. Darryl Franklin stood there, glancing at nothing in particular. "Good morning," he said when his gaze reached her again.

"Good morning," she replied. Should she ask him inside? She wasn't certain.

It was then Maggie appeared beside her. "Come in, come in," Maggie said enthusiastically, ushering Darryl through the door at the same time.

"The kettle is boiling. Let me get you a coffee." She didn't wait for an answer, but ushered him into a chair in the sitting room. Maggie was gone before he had a chance to protest. He'd opened his mouth to do so, but then closed it moments later.

When Maggie returned, she carried a wooden tray. It was filled with coffee for Darryl, and tea for the women. It also held a number of freshly baked muffins. The aroma was amazing.

"I can't possibly," Darryl said when Maggie offered him muffins. "I've already eaten," he added.

Maggie glanced at the clock. "Knowing you, that was hours ago. Take a muffin or two. Or three if you want."

Hun watched the grin that crept across his face. "You know me well. Too well, if truth be told," he said, then chuckled. He reached out and took a blueberry muffin. It wasn't long and it was gone.

Hun liked a man who enjoyed his food, and it seemed that described Darryl well. *Wait.* How did she know that? She closed her eyes briefly, but quickly opened them again. Tiny snippets of her life seemed to be creeping into her mind. At least that's what she thought they were.

"Moments before you arrived, I told Hun she should go for a walk. The fresh air will do her good. You could accompany her. " Maggie lifted her eyebrows as if challenging him to refuse.

"You don't have to, Darryl," Hun said, not wanting him to feel obligated.

He grinned then. "Is that the price of a coffee and muffin today?" he said, almost laughing. "I would be delighted." He turned to Hun then. "Do you have a warm coat and gloves?"

"I…I don't know," she answered, feeling somewhat disappointed. She was looking forward to going outside.

"I'm almost certain you'll find them in your closet," Maggie told her. "If not, you can borrow mine. We're about the same size."

Hun sipped her tea, warmth filling her. Not from the tea, but from these people, these strangers looking out for her. She didn't know who she was, but it didn't seem to bother them. They both treated her like a friend, someone they'd known for years. No matter her memory was shot, Hun couldn't remember feeling this way before.

Before. In her former life. The one she couldn't remember anything about.

Hun needed to know – she wanted to know who she was. Until then, her thoughts of herself would remain sullied. Her mind kept coming back to her being a soiled dove.

And that was the last thing she wanted to know about herself.

~*~

"It's a small town, but a good one," Darryl told her as they wandered about. Her arm hooked through his felt…nice. Darryl was a good man, Maggie told her so, and Hun had found it out for herself.

"Were you born here?" she asked, out of curiosity than anything else.

Darryl studied her momentarily before answering. Did he think her question strange? "No, but sometimes it feels like I was. Everyone here treats me like one of their own."

If she stayed, would they do the same for her? Through her confusion, Hun wondered if she could ever feel part of a community again. If her identity was not discovered, where would she be then? She preferred not to think about it.

As they went from store to store, window shopping, Darryl told her about each of the owners, and how long they'd owned their respective stores. He also told her what they sold. She stopped out the front of the dressmaker's store. The gowns in the window were beautiful.

The thought had her feeling guilty. The clothes she'd inherited from Daisy, Maggie's former boarder, were lovely, and were a perfect fit for her. Why did she feel like something was missing? Because it was, and she knew it. The clothes didn't belong to her. It almost felt as though she had taken on another person's identity.

She shook herself mentally. What a silly thought! Then again, she didn't have her own identity, which left her feeling empty. Still, she shouldn't wish for something that couldn't be satisfied. Daisy, it turns out, was a thief. Hun certainly didn't want to be thought of as a common thief.

Truth be told, she could be, but no one knew, not even Hun herself. Oh, how she longed to know exactly who she was, and what sort of life she led.

When she glanced up, Sheriff Dodd was waving at them. "Wait up," he called from across the other side of the road. He strolled leisurely toward them. The moment he was close to the pair, he spoke. "I've made some enquiries with the marshals. I hope to hear back in a day or two."

Hun was disappointed. She'd hoped the sheriff had good news – that he knew who she was. Unfortunately it wasn't the case.

"Thank you, Sheriff," Darryl said.

Hun smiled. There was nothing to add. Besides she didn't want the sheriff, or Darryl for that matter, to see her disappointment.

Still, it was early days, and she knew his investigation would be ongoing. There was nothing for anyone to do, so Darryl continued to walk with her, and show Hun around town. As much as she liked Maggie, she couldn't deny enjoying Darryl's company.

Chapter Ten

Two days passed, and still no news. Darryl rode into town each day to check if there was any news.

Nothing new had been learned, which he found disappointing. He was certain Hun would be frustrated. If only the sheriff had learned who she was, it wouldn't be so bad for her.

Maggie had invited him to join them for lunch each day, which he accepted. Being in town meant he could be kept appraised of the situation. He also enjoyed the daily walks he and Hun had after their meal.

Except now the weather was mostly unpredictable. It was becoming far too cold for either of them to stroll around town. Christmas was almost upon them. He wondered how the mysterious woman could enjoy the Christmas celebrations while not knowing her identity.

The three were in the sitting room sipping their hot beverages, and talking about nothing in particular. Maggie announced she would like Darryl to join them for Christmas, since he was alone. "I'm not always by myself for Christmas," Darryl told her. "Mostly, I've been invited to various places."

Maggie almost chuckled. "By the parents of spinsters, do you mean?" she asked, then laughed. They both knew it was true. There weren't a lot of eligible women in town, and the same applied to the men.

Darryl rolled his eyes. "At least I can refuse this year," he said flatly. "It's not fun going to someone's home, knowing they expect a marriage proposal for their daughter in return." He shook his head. "It is frustrating to say the least."

Before he could say another word, there was a knock at the door. Maggie placed her mug of tea on the side table and went to the door. The voices were muffled, and then stopped. Maggie brought the visitor inside out of the cold.

"Sheriff Dodd would like to speak with you, Hun," Maggie said. "We'll leave you two alone."

Darryl stood, but Hun waved him down. "I'd rather you both stayed. My memory is so bad, I'll probably forget whatever the sheriff tells me."

"Coffee, Sheriff?" she offered, but he turned her down.

"This won't take long," he said. "I have some news. This is not official, mind," he added. "It's today's newspaper, but I'm still waiting for confirmation." He opened the newspaper he held in his hands.

"What is it, Sheriff Dodd? What does it say?" Hun's words were urgent. She was so desperate to put all the pieces together.

He leaned forward and showed them the article in the newspaper. "This looks like you. At least I think it does." He laid it on the side table, and invited them to check it out.

Darryl stared at the photograph. Although it was rather scratchy, he could make out it was indeed their visitor, Hun. His eyes scanned the article. A few words stood out – *missing, kidnapped,* and *bank robbery*. How did they relate to the woman standing near to him.

"May I?" he asked the sheriff, who nodded his agreement. Hun sat back in her chair, she was looking rather pale. "Are you happy for me to read this in the kitchen, then return?" he asked her. It was hard to concentrate with all the eyes on him.

"Of course," she whispered.

Darryl quickly left the room. Sitting at the table, he carefully read the information. The headline left no doubt about what had happened. *Bank Hostage Missing, Feared Dead.*

She was a hostage in a bank robbery. But why would a bank robber take the hostage, then place them in a box? Darryl's heart thudded. He already knew the reason. Doing so would mean there would be no witness to testify against him. According to the article, the bank clerk was killed, and there were no other customers in the bank at the time. Except for Hun. Velma Wooten, that is.

Working at the mercantile, Velma was depositing the day's takings when she walked in on a bank robbery. It was as simple and as complicated as that. Dragging her out of the bank, the robber had to dispose of her somehow, and rode away with her. Velma was never seen again.

Until now.

Darryl had to tell her the truth. It might answer some questions for her, but it might also put her in added danger if the bank robber found out she was still alive. It was a delicate situation she found herself in.

He closed the newspaper and returned to the sitting room. Sitting next to her, he turned to Velma, then held her hand. "Your name is Velma Wooten," he said gently.

She gasped. "Velma Wooten," she repeated, surprise on her face. "It doesn't sound familiar."

Was that possible? Could a person have their memory completely wiped because of trauma? He turned to the sheriff. "I think Doc Spencer should be here."

Sheriff Dodd nodded. "Good idea. I'll get him." Moments later he was gone.

"I'll make a fresh tea for you, my dear," Maggie said. She appeared as pale as Velma.

Darryl was about to offer to do it instead, but Velma clutched his hands tightly. She seemed terrified of what he was about to say. By the time Maggie came back with fresh drinks for them all, the sheriff had arrived with Doc Spencer.

The doc stood to the side, along with Sheriff Dodd. He nodded to Darryl, urging him to go ahead and provide the rest of the information. "Velma," he said gently, "according to this article, you were at the *Helena National Bank* when it was robbed."

She gasped, and the doc stepped forward. Darryl studied her face. Although Velma was pale, she was no worse than when he showed her the photograph of herself.

"The article has you listed as a missing person," he said, and she gasped again. "I don't know how to tell you this…" He paused, not wanting to upset her further, but it needed to be said. She deserved to know the truth. Was entitled to the full story. He shook his head briefly, then continued. "You were taken hostage by the bank robber, and have not been seen since."

Except she had. Velma was delivered to him. He'd saved her life, but only by default. Anyone could have found her, but if Darryl hadn't opened that box in time, she would be dead. A shudder went through him. How did anyone do such a thing to another human? He had questioned this before, but now the full story had been told, it was even harder to believe.

"We need to work out a plan to keep you safe, Miss Wooten," Sheriff Dodd told her.

Velma nodded slightly. "Do you think they'll come after me again?" The moment the words were out of her mouth, she began to hyperventilate. Doc Spencer stepped forward, and Darryl moved out of his way.

"Breathe slowly," he told her. "Like this." He demonstrated and Velma followed suit. After a few minutes her panic subsided. He looked into her face, then checked her eyes. "You look tired," he said. "Are you sleeping?"

Velma glanced up at Darryl. "Not really," she said. "What if he finds me and puts me in that box again?" Her words tore at Darryl's heart.

It was then the doc opened his medical bag. "This is Laudanum. Take a few drops before bed," he said.

"It will help you sleep." He snapped his bag closed, and stood once more.

Darryl handed the newspaper back to Sheriff Dodd. "Could I speak with you, Sheriff? In your office?"

The sheriff's poker face didn't change. "Of course," he said, then the two men left the boarding house.

They needed to work out a plan. Velma would be a target, especially if the kidnapper discovered she was still alive and where she was living.

Chapter Eleven

The moment the truth was revealed, Velma began to panic. At least now she knew who she was, but the truth scared her. Being taken hostage by a bank robber was beyond anything she could imagine. Being secured in that box? It was obviously the robber's way of ridding themselves of her and any testimony she could make.

Darryl's fingers wrapped around hers, and although it was comforting, Velma couldn't stop herself from breathing rapidly. It was a panic attack, she knew it was, but that didn't mean she could stop it. A gentle squeeze from the man who saved her life didn't help, despite the compassionate expression on his face.

If she couldn't control her breathing, Velma knew she would pass out. It was the last thing she wanted.

Darryl's fingers slipped away from hers, and moments later, Doc Spencer was standing in front of her. As much as the man was kind, she felt safe with Darryl. It didn't take long, and the doc had helped Velma control her breathing.

It was all too much. One minute she didn't know who she was. The next she is declared a missing person. A hostage in a bank robbery no less.

The target of a killer.

Velma's heart pounded. Her head ached, and then it was spinning. Doc Spencer was holding something up in front of her. She heard Darryl's voice. It seemed far away. Then the world went black.

"Velma? Hun?" Maggie's voice hovered above her, but the hand that held hers was not that of a woman. It was far too large.

"Velma, it's Darryl. Open your eyes." His voice was beside her. Whispering softly in her ear. Confusion surrounded her, but she opened her eyes anyway. "Let me sit you up," Darryl said gently.

She stared into his face. "Where…where am I?" she asked, still in a state of confusion. Her mind was in turmoil, unsure where she was.

"You're safe," Darryl told her. "You fainted, not surprisingly. It was a lot to take in."

A lot to take in? What did that mean? Velma's mind went back to the discussion earlier. Everything was a fog. She recalled a newspaper, and Darryl leaving the room. To read an article? She closed her eyes trying to sort it all out in her mind. "Bank robbery," she whispered without knowing why she'd said it.

Darryl studied her. "Yes, you got caught up in a bank robbery."

Her heart pounded. "I robbed a bank?" she whispered, not wanting to say it out loud.

"No. You didn't rob a bank. You were an innocent victim, and were taken hostage in the midst of a bank robbery.

Relief filled her. Of all the scenarios she'd thought might be part of her life, bank robber was not one of them. "Praise the Lord," Velma said, her voice full of emotion.

Darryl glanced up. It was then she noticed Doc Spencer. "I want you to take the Laudanum now. You've had a traumatic experience. It will calm you down."

She did what the doc suggested – he knew better than Velma. It would be foolish not to listen to him. The doctor stepped back once she'd taken the medicine, and Maggie stepped forward. She had a mug of tea in her hands.

If things weren't so serious, Velma would have laughed. Velma appreciated it, she really did. She was learning that Maggie's answer to everything was a cup of tea. "Thank you, Maggie," she said, and sipped the tea. As it slid down her throat, it did make her feel a little better. Was it because she was focusing on something else? She would probably never know.

What she did know was these people, these strangers, were worried about her. Here in Hopetoun, they were a community. Not that she'd met a lot of the townsfolk, but she'd met enough of them to know. They would look out for her. Heck, they already had.

It was amidst these thoughts the truth hit her. "The robber put me in the box to kill me?" Velma knew she shouldn't be surprised. He wanted, needed, to eliminate any witnesses, and that's exactly what she was. Apparently. She closed her eyes and a scene flashed into her mind. It was a man holding a gun, a bandana covering much of his face.

The vision was gone almost as soon as it had appeared. She gasped. "He shot the bank teller," she whispered, her voice breaking as she spoke.

Her hands were shaking, and Darryl took the mug of tea from her and put it on a side table. "The teller was shot," he said gently. "Unfortunately the man died."

Tears sprung to her eyes. Not only was she a hostage in a bank robbery, she was a witness to a murder. Things surely couldn't get any worse.

~*~

With her arm hooked through Darryl's she felt safe again. Velma needed fresh air, and Darryl offered to take a stroll with her. At first she was reluctant. What if the robber was here in town? Both the sheriff and Darryl reassured her there was no way he could know where she was. Until a short time ago, no one knew her identity. That being the case, how could her abductor find her?

Besides, as Darryl pointed out to her, only a handful of people knew who she really was. They were the same people who she'd met and dealt with. Other townsfolk might have seen her, but hadn't met her. Or been introduced in any way. His explanation was valid, and it helped Velma to relax. At least a little.

She was rugged up in Daisy's thick coat, and had one of her knitted scarves around her neck. Velma enjoyed her walks with Darryl – she was becoming more enamored to him each day. The last thing she wanted was to have feelings for a man she'd only recently met. Especially given her current circumstances.

It was then a thought occurred to her. Was she putting his life in danger? She shook herself mentally. Perhaps she should keep her distance from the wainwright. Let him get on with his work instead of pulling him away from it every day.

Mind you, he wasn't complaining, she noted. Darryl seemed more than happy to accompany her on her daily strolls. Truth be told, she wouldn't venture outside without him by her side.

Velma pulled her gloved hand away.

Darryl stopped walking. "Is there a problem?" he asked gently.

She shook her head slightly, but felt the opposite. "I'm putting you in danger," she said quietly. "You saved my life, and this is how I repay you." If he hadn't held her hand so tightly, Velma would have run back to the boarding house and Maggie.

Instead, she stood facing Darryl. He was frowning. Moments later his expression changed and he brought her hand to his lips. "I would do anything for you, Velma," he whispered. "I've become very fond of you."

His words filled Velma with warmth. She wanted to tell him how she felt, but right now didn't seem like the right time to do so. Especially since people were doing the same thing they were – strolling along the boardwalk before the weather became worse.

"We should probably head back to the boarding house," Darryl said. "We both know Maggie doesn't like tardiness when it comes to meals."

He was right. Maggie went to a lot of trouble, and they shouldn't keep her waiting. She slipped her hand back through his arm, and once again, Velma felt safe. More than that, Darryl made her feel as though she was special.

As though she was someone who deserved her place in the world.

73

Chapter Twelve

"The meal was delicious as always, Maggie. Thank you," Darryl said as he wiped his mouth. "You really are spoiling me."

Maggie chuckled. "It is you who is spoiling the two of us. We get tired of our own company sometimes. Do you agree, Velma?"

His eyes went to Velma, who glanced across and smiled at him. A shiver went down his spine. How could that be? A mere smile. They weren't touching, they weren't even sitting close together. And yet…

"I most certainly do," Velma said. Her demeanor had changed since their walk. After finding out the details of her abduction, she was petrified. Even on their stroll, Velma seemed rather stressed. Since arriving back at the boarding house, she seemed to have settled somewhat.

Darryl could totally understand why. The man had tried to murder Velma to keep her quiet. The thought shattered his heart. Why he felt this way, Darryl had no idea. Or perhaps he did. He'd grown fond of Velma, but until recently, he didn't know her. And due to the circumstances, he still didn't know her. Except he'd learned she was a wonderful woman who cared about others.

She might be a mystery to everyone she'd met since landing in Hopetoun, but the truth was slowly being revealed. He hoped that meant her memory would come back to her in due course.

"I suppose I should go," Darryl announced, although he really didn't want to leave. Any excuse would see him staying, and yet, he knew he needed to leave. Velma was getting under his skin. When he was with her, he was happy and content. The times they were apart, all he did was think about her.

Darryl shook himself mentally. Velma was not a person to get involved with. She had her own set of problems, and if he started a relationship with her, they would become his problems. Except the truth was, he was already mixed up in her situation. Not through any fault of his own. Or hers.

Like Velma, he was an innocent victim in all this. He would still like to know why he received the box with her inside. It seemed the strangest thing.

He certainly didn't know any bank robbers. The puzzle had him complexed.

"Why don't you stay awhile longer?" Maggie asked him. "I'll bring coffee into the sitting room. You two go ahead."

Not that she'd given him any reason to think so, but Darryl wondered if Maggie was playing matchmaker. It seemed a strange thing to do. Especially given Velma had only today found out who she was, and what had caused her to be in that box.

Darryl stood, and Velma followed suit. They walked together, and Darryl offered her the chair closest to the fire. Outside it was icy cold. He didn't look forward to the ride back home, but a little longer here in the warmth wouldn't hurt. His horse was being well looked after at the livery, so there really was no reason to leave now.

"How is your work on the wagon going?" Velma asked. He decided she was trying to fill the silence. It wasn't like they needed to talk. They'd never had an uncomfortable silence between them. When they strolled around town, they barely spoke – simply enjoyed their time together.

"It's going well," Darryl answered. "There's not a lot left to do. If I put the time in, I could finish it in the next few days." Except he didn't want to do that. Darryl didn't want to admit it, not even to himself, but he'd rather spend his spare time with Velma. Not finishing up a wagon that wasn't due until mid-January. Even as he thought about it, Velma seemed sad about the situation. Did she realize if he spent more time on the wagon, that was less time with her?

"You're still coming here for Christmas, aren't you?" she asked, and Darryl flinched. He hadn't given Maggie a firm answer, but he had no reason not to accept. There were several options normally open to him, but most were from the parents of women he had no interest in.

"He's coming here, aren't you, Darryl?" Maggie said as she sauntered into the room holding a tray. She handed him a mug of steaming coffee, then offered him cake.

"I really can't eat any more," Darryl said tapping his belly and ignoring the question. He brought the coffee to his lips and sipped.

"Don't ignore my question. At least my invitation doesn't include pressure to marry someone you're not interested in." Maggie grinned, and Velma turned a deep shade of red.

"If you're not doing it out of pity…?" He took another sip of coffee then glanced up at Maggie who was scowling at him. "Thank you. I accept your invitation. What can I bring?"

Maggie shook her head. "Absolutely nothing. Except a happy demeanor."

That he could do. Especially if Velma would be there, which he knew she would.

~*~

By the time he left the boarding house, the snow was heavier. He was rugged up well, so Darryl was not cold. It was his horse he worried about. The sooner they arrived home, the better. For both of them.

Thankfully, his property wasn't far away. In better weather, he could walk there in a reasonably short time, but not this time of year.

Darryl was relieved when they arrived home, and immediately took his horse into the stables. As he brushed him down, he pondered Maggie's invitation.

Had she noticed he was drawn to Velma? Even at the very start? At first he believed it was due to her situation. He certainly felt bad for her. Darryl even pitied her. But now it was different. He'd come to know her, and liked who she was. Even before Velma knew her name, he had feelings for her, but had to rein those feelings in. Not only for her benefit, but also for his own.

The number of hours he worked didn't make him good husband material. He knew that more than anyone. He also knew he worked longer to fill in his days, and sometimes his nights. Was that the reason he was pressured by the townsfolk to marry? He would probably never know.

Shaking his head, Darryl tried to put the quandary out of his mind. After all, he wasn't interested in getting married. Not to anyone.

He was happily single, except for the lack of good food. The thought sent his mind in a different direction, and he wondered if Velma could cook.

Chapter Thirteen

Velma felt deflated the moment Darryl left. She wasn't sure why, except she had become rather fond of him.

She was certain it was because he was the one who saved her. She'd heard about it happening in these circumstances, and tried to put Darryl out of her mind. Except she couldn't. He was there in her waking hours, and also when she tried to sleep.

Even with the Laudanum, her sleep was fitful. The dark circles under her eyes bore testament to it. Maggie had been a good friend to her, and Velma knew she couldn't ask for anyone better. Staying there at the boarding house was only temporary, she knew, but where would she go after that?

Another thought crossed her mind, and Velma wished she could stop thinking about the way in which she arrived here. Except she couldn't. What if the bank robber decided he needed to ensure she was dead? Would he be able to pinpoint her to living here in Hopetoun?

Her heart sank. Perhaps the best thing for Maggie, and the others who helped her, was to move on. Except she still had no proof of identity except the newspaper article. What bank manager would hand her money on the strength of an article? She was stuck here whether she liked it or not.

Truth be told, she did like it here. Except she didn't like putting her friends in danger. And they were her friends. Velma may not have been here long, but she felt part of the community. They'd taken her under their wings, and looked out for her. She couldn't ask for more than that.

If she had the choice, Velma would choose to stay in this lovely little town for the rest of her life. She sighed. She had a whole other life back in Helena. At least that's what she had been told, and she had to believe it.

Working for the mercantile, the article said, which meant she wasn't a soiled dove. Her heart hammered in her chest at the relief she felt.

Her head was spinning with questions. Velma wanted to know everything about her life. Were her parents alive? Did she have siblings? Was she married or single?

Glancing down at her left hand, there was no ring there, so she assumed she was single. Except she knew it was possible the bank robber could have stolen it.

"You're pale." Maggie's voice brought her out of her turmoil. It was a blessed relief. The article had brought up more questions than answers. It made her feel worse than before, when she didn't know her name. "Are you feeling alright?" Maggie asked as she sat down beside her.

Velma shook her head. "Who am I?" she whispered, then closed her eyes against the world. A hand reached out and held hers, and she knew Maggie was there for her.

"I can't imagine being in your shoes," Maggie said, her words comforting, even though she had no answers.

Velma fought against the tears that threatened to fall. "I don't know if there's anyone back in Helena who is worried about me. Concerned about where I am." She shook her head briefly, then opened her eyes.

Maggie seemed worried. About her? She leaned in and placed an arm around Velma, pulling her into a hug. "I'm sure Sheriff Dodd can find out for you. Don't make yourself ill over it."

The words made Velma feel better. For only a moment. "What if he makes those inquiries, and the person who tried to kill me finds out. They'll work out where I am." This time the tears did fall. Not for herself, but for Maggie and the others who had looked after her.

The entire situation was a mess. A dangerous mess, and Velma wasn't prepared to put all their lives in danger to save herself.

This time Maggie pulled her into a full hug. The sort of hug that made you feel loved and wanted. A hug you never wanted to end. Except Velma knew it would have to end sometime soon. Maggie had work to do, and she was keeping the boarding house owner away from her work.

Having Velma there was a distraction. She swallowed down hard. Did her presence also put the older woman in danger? Emotion overwhelmed Velma, and she pulled away. "I'm going to lay down if that's alright?" she asked. "I'm feeling rather drained."

Maggie stared into her face. Was she trying to determine if Velma was lying to her? For the most part, it was true. She was totally drained – it had been a difficult day. Although Velma knew she should be ecstatic. Finally she knew who she was, and where she lived. Except it hadn't made her feel better. Instead it made her feel worse. Worried, and scared for her new friends.

She went into her room and sat down at the chair near the window. It had become a favorite spot for Velma. Watching out the window at people going about their business seemed to lift her spirits. Only now it didn't. Instead she felt guilt-ridden. Was she putting all these people in danger?

If only she could withdraw some of her money from the bank. It would be her means of escape. She could get the train out of town, and go goodness knew where. If she were honest with herself, Velma didn't want to leave Hopetoun. She didn't want to leave Maggie or Darryl.

Except she really had no choice. If the man who tried to kill her found out Velma was still alive, he would come after her. There was nothing more certain.

Tears rolling down her face, Velma prepared herself to leave. None of the clothing was hers, which meant there was nothing to pack. She wiped at her tears, then splashed cold water on her face. "I'm going for a walk," she told Maggie, keeping her face averted. "I won't be long."

Maggie stared at her. "Do you want company?" she asked wiping her hands on her apron.

Velma's heart hammered. Company was the last thing she wanted. "I'll be fine," she said. "It's not like I can get lost." She chuckled despite not feeling joyful. Maggie stared at Velma, but didn't say a word.

She pulled on the thick coat left behind when Daisy had fled town, and wrapped the warm scarf around her neck. Snatching up the newspaper the sheriff had left behind, she headed to the bank. Would the article be enough for the bank manager to provide her with funds? As much as she hoped it would be, Velma wasn't holding her breath.

Resolving to ensure she secured her funds from the bank, Velma straightened her shoulders and opened the heavy door. She stepped inside, her heart hammering and the newspaper under her arm.

Chapter Fourteen

Darryl was busy working on the commissioned wagon. In the winter, his workshop was bitterly cold. He couldn't risk having a fire in there in case any embers got away. With so much timber packed into the huge workspace, it wasn't worth the risk.

In the summer, it was a completely different story. He normally left the large doors open, to keep the area cool. For now, with the workshop bitterly cold, he sanded the large wagon with his gloves on. It wasn't ideal, he knew, but he had been doing this work for all of his working life, and was used to it.

"Darryl," a voice called. "Are you there?" He could barely hear the words, but they were spoken urgently. It sounded like Sheriff Dodd.

He put down his tools, and opened the large doors. "Is everything alright, Sheriff?" he asked. His heart pounded as he instinctively knew this would be about Velma. "Is Velma…"

Darryl didn't get to finish the sentence, as the sheriff interrupted him. "Honestly, I don't know," he said, pushing his hat back on his head. "She's disappeared."

Disappeared? How could that be? Instead of voicing his thoughts, Darryl stared at the sheriff. He shook his head, trying to make sense of it all. "She has no money," he said, frowning. "Where could she go? She has no money." That was when it hit him. "Was she…" He took a deep breath as he studied the sheriff. "…snatched?" Not that he would admit it to the sheriff, but Darryl was concerned. He was more than a little worried for her.

Sheriff Dodd pulled his hat from his head. "She had money. I spoke to the bank manager, and he gave her ten dollars. Said the article was enough proof of who she was." Running his fingers through his hair, the sheriff seemed perplexed. "I was hoping she came out here."

"I wish she had. It would be safer than wandering about on her own."

"Well, I ain't going to find her standing here talking with you. I'll keep moving," Sheriff Dodd told him. He slammed his hat on his head, and headed back to his horse.

"Sheriff, wait," Darryl called. "I'll come with you. I feel responsible for her."

Sheriff Dodd put a hand to his shoulder. "She is not your responsibility. Miss Wooten is free to go wherever she wants, whenever she wishes."

Although he knew the sheriff was right, Darryl still felt liable for Velma's safety. Once he knew who she was, and the reason for her landing here in the most unconventional way, he should have taken charge of her safety. "What if the bank robber is still after her?" Darryl felt hollow just saying the words. It was highly likely she had a target on her back.

Sheriff Dodd stared at him for long moments before speaking. Darryl held his breath the entire time, waiting for an answer. "In my opinion," he said slowly, "it is highly likely he will. Velma is a witness to his crime. A victim, but also a star witness." Peter Dodd pulled his hat off his head and scratched it. "I'm about to go searching for her, but I thought you'd want to know."

Of course he did! Darryl saved her life for goodness sake. He had no intention of letting an ornery bank robber get his way and kill Velma, an eyewitness to his crimes.

It didn't get past him that around a week ago, he didn't know Velma. His life was peaceful and without drama. Instead, every day was filled with news from the sheriff, news articles proclaiming the unknown woman as Velma Wooten, and now, the fact she'd run off.

His head spinning with the news, Darryl tried to sort out in his mind where she could go. Where she would go. With little money, and little knowledge of the area, she would be a sitting duck. "I'm coming too," Darryl said firmly.

Glancing at the sheriff, Darryl knew the other man was studying him. "My deputy is already looking, but I won't refuse the additional help." He patted his horse and led him to water while Darryl saddled his horse, ready to search.

What he would do if they didn't find Velma, he didn't know. It was difficult to admit, but Velma had become the center of his world.

He and the sheriff rode back into town together, mostly in silence. In his mind, Darryl relived the places he'd taken Velma to on their daily walks. One of her favorite places to visit was the gardens. They were bordering the town, and didn't take long to get there, but provided cover. She could easily hide there if necessary. Had he told her that much during their walks?

Darryl's mind was whirling. Did it mean he'd inadvertently convinced her to run? To hide? His heart hammered in his chest. It was the last thing he wanted to do. Velma needed protection, not a fool like him to convince her to hide. Especially in this inclement weather. She could freeze to death.

No, she wouldn't be so foolish, he was certain. He needed to clear his mind of his emotions, and think laterally. If he were in her shoes, where would he go? *Think, Darryl, think!* Almost the moment his mind cleared, he heard the train whistle. It heralded the train about to arrive at the station. Heart pounding, Darryl knew that's where they would find her.

"Train station," he called to the sheriff, and both men headed that way. Horses galloping, Darryl knew they had little time. The moment all baggage was loaded, and deliveries unloaded, the train would leave the station for its next destination.

With Velma aboard.

Time was precious. They had to get there before she could leave. Before the bank robber, Butch Carpenter, aka Butch the Assassin, the sheriff said his name was, got to her first. Darryl hoped and prayed the man had no clue where she was, but he knew what train line he shipped her off too. Covering his bases, he would check every town, big and small, if he had even an inkling Velma was still alive.

The odds of that happening were small, but it was still a possibility. As they arrived at the station, Darryl jumped from his horse. There was no time to secure him. Besides, Darryl knew he wouldn't leave. Sheriff Dodd followed suit.

The station was bustling. Probably the busiest Darryl had ever seen it. Porters were carrying baggage for travelers, and passengers were boarding the train. There! He spotted Velma, and ran toward her as she headed into the carriage, ready to board.

He ran faster than he ever had, and reached out, putting his hand firmly to her shoulder. "Velma," he said urgently. When she turned to face him, it wasn't her. Wasn't Velma. "I apologize, Ma'am," he told the stranger. "I was looking for a friend."

She nodded curtly, and continued to board.

Glancing about, Darryl was terrified it was too late. Had Butch Carpenter already snatched Velma? Killed her? He swallowed down the emotions that threatened to overtake him. He had a job to do, and that was save Velma from her would-be killer. And herself.

The train whistle sounded again. It was almost time for the train to leave. Steam, smoke and particles of coal covered the platform as the driver readied to depart. Darryl couldn't see a thing. The train itself was barely visible.

The platform was suddenly silent. The passengers were aboard the train, those sending them on their way had left. Through the smoke and dust from the coal, he saw nothing, but he heard a sound. A woman's voice. Trying to scream?

His heart beat accelerated. It beat not only in his chest but in his head, making it difficult to think. There it was again. The sound was more of a squeak than a scream, but it was definitely there. He heard the shuffling of feet, and ran toward the sound, his gun in hand. He had no doubt the would-be kidnapper would have the intention of killing Velma before she had a chance to testify.

As the smoke began to clear, he saw them. Butch Carpenter had an arm around Velma, and not in a good way. His arm straddled her waist, and he held her tightly, pulling her along. She was pale and disheveled, and it broke his heart.

As much as Darryl tried to deny his feelings for the previously unknown woman, he knew he was in love with Velma. He had to save her from this fiend. This would-be murderer.

He'd endeavored to kill Velma once before, and was attempting it again. It surprised him Butch Carpenter was doing so in public. Then again, he was desperate and had nothing to lose. Law enforcement had been after him for a long time, according to Sheriff Dodd.

He aimed his gun at the other man's head. If he pulled the trigger, no one would worry. The outlaw was a killer and a bank robber. The scum of the earth.

Except that wasn't Darryl. He'd rather see the man in jail, or more likely, hang for his crimes. Killing him was too easy. For Butch Carpenter.

It was then he noticed Sheriff Dodd was nowhere to be seen. Darryl didn't dare take his eyes away from the scene playing out in front of him. One wrong move, and he'd be dead. And so would Velma. As the train began to pull away, he saw it.

Sheriff Dodd quietly came up behind Butch Carpenter and put his gun to the outlaw's head. "Drop the gun and let the woman go," he demanded. Butch Carpenter laughed.

The train whistle sounded again, and the platform was completely covered in smoke. Darryl couldn't see a thing.

By the time it cleared, Butch Carpenter was gone, and Velma was in a heap on the ground.

Chapter Fifteen

Velma was both dazed and confused. One minute she was being held hostage by the outlaw who had already tried to kill her once, and the next she was lying on the cold ground.

Smoke surrounded her. She could see nothing through the haze, and it felt as though she was choking. Velma couldn't stop coughing.

Moments later she was being lifted from the cold and hard ground. The train whistle blew again, and the train was moving. She couldn't see it, but she could hear it chugging out of the station. Without her.

"Velma," Darryl said quietly. "You are safe. He's gone."

The man who tried to kill her was gone? How could that be? He'd told Velma she stood between him and freedom, and the only way he could survive was to eliminate her.

Eliminate.

What he really meant was murder her. Velma swallowed back the emotion that now overwhelmed her, except it didn't work. Too much had happened in such a short time, and she could no longer pretend everything was alright.

Because it wasn't.

Darryl held her close. He was whispering in her ear. Reassuring her, promising to keep her safe from harm. Velma wasn't convinced he could do that. The outlaw now knew she was in Hopetoun. It pained her to think it, but he wouldn't leave until she was dead.

And no longer a problem to him.

Darryl carried her across the platform, and outside to where his horse was hitched. Sheriff Dodd was by his side, gun at the ready. Velma watched as the sheriff scoured the area, checking for the outlaw.

The man who wanted her dead.

Her mind was racing. Velma didn't know what to think, or what she should do. It was all too hard. Instead of thinking, she rested her head against Darryl's chest and closed her eyes. That was when he whispered in her ear. "I love you, Velma. I couldn't bear to lose you."

Darryl's arms tightened around her. Velma was not unhappy about his revelation. She had feelings for her rescuer, and desperately wanted to tell him so.

Only now, she was coughing more each time she opened her mouth. "I'm taking you to the doc," Darryl said firmly, not giving her a chance to protest. "It's not far."

Instead of placing her on his horse, as Velma anticipated, he carried her all the way there. Doc Spencer was quick to react. "How much smoke did she inhale?" he asked as Darryl placed her on the doc's treatment bed.

"A lot," Darryl said as Velma continued to cough. She felt something placed over her face, and the coughing began to ease.

"Oxygen," Doc Spencer said. "It's a new fangled invention, but said to work well in these situations.

Velma felt a hand over hers, and knew it was Darryl. His mere presence was comforting. How could she have even thought about leaving him? The answer was clear – she was afraid for his safety, when this entire time, he was fearful for her.

Velma felt far better after being on the oxygen for some time. How long that was, she wasn't sure. The entire time, Darryl didn't leave her side, even when the doc suggested it could take a while. Finally, the mask was removed from her face, and she was allowed to sit up. The pungent odor of smoke filled her nostrils. Panic began to set in. Was the outlaw back and trying to kill her again?

She was breathing fast, way too fast, but Velma couldn't stop herself. "Velma," Darryl whispered. "Slow your breathing. You're safe here." His arm went up around her shoulders, and she felt comforted.

"Smoke," she said between panting. "I can smell it."

Darryl caressed her cheek. "It's in our clothes. There is no fire here, and definitely no smoke."

She collapsed against his chest in relief. Velma didn't know what she would have done without him. Darryl was always there when she needed him. How could she ever repay him? Velma knew she couldn't. It wouldn't matter what she did, his kindness and his heroism could never truly be repaid.

"If you feel up to it, you can go home now, Velma." Doc Spencer's words brought her joy. Until the words sunk in. She had no home. Not here in Hopetoun. She was a stranger to this place. Only a few of the townsfolk even knew she existed. Velma shook her head. She wanted to blurt out the truth about her situation. Hopetoun was not home, not really.

On the other hand, the article said she was from Helena. That wasn't home either. Did that mean she was destitute? Except that was a person with no home and no money. The bank manager gave her a small amount of money to tide her over until she could get back *home*.

There was that word again. Home. "I have no home," she whispered, and the two men stared at her.

"There could still be some confusion," Doc Spencer said. "Keep an eye on her." He then held her hand and helped Velma to the floor.

She wasn't confused. Was she? Maybe she was but didn't realize it. With all she'd been through lately, nothing would surprise her. One thing Velma did know, and that was she wanted a hot bath to wash away the smell of smoke. Not to mention the stench that came from the man trying to kill her.

Chapter Sixteen

Darryl could see the confusion on Velma's face as clearly as Doc Spencer could. Not that he was surprised. So much had happened to her recently. Anyone in the same situation would feel the same, he was certain.

"I'll take you back to the boarding house," he said. "I'm sure Maggie can organise a hot bath for you. That and fresh clothes, and you'll feel like new again." Only Darryl knew it was a lie. Things needed to change for her to feel better. Mostly, Butch Carpenter needed to be captured and tried for his actions.

Surely attempting to murder the same person twice came with a much heavier penalty. Not to mention the teller he'd shot and killed in the course of the bank robbery. Or the money he'd stolen.

He lifted Velma off her feet and headed toward the front door of the doctor's office. "I can walk," she whispered.

Of course he knew that, but she had to be weak from her attack. Besides, it felt good holding her in his arms. "And I can carry you," he growled. Was she annoyed with him? Opening the front door, Darryl glanced about. He saw no sign of Butch Carpenter, and hoped that meant he'd left town. Unfortunately, he couldn't be certain that would be the case. "Besides, it's not far." He carried her along the boardwalk, making his way to the boarding house.

The front door opened before he even had a chance to knock.

"Oh my goodness," Maggie said urgently. "Are you hurt? I heard what happened?" Tears sprung to the other woman's eyes. With his hands full, Darryl could do nothing to comfort her.

"Velma is fine," he said, keeping his voice calm. "Her voice is a little scratchy, but she's asked for a hot bath."

Maggie stared at Velma as she swiped at the errant tears. Darryl should have known Maggie would be upset. The two women had become quite close since Velma had arrived in town. Moving inside, he placed Velma on one of the comfortable chairs, and stood by her side.

He was afraid to leave her alone. What if Butch Carpenter was watching their every move? What if he broke in during the night and once again attempted to murder Velma. His heart hammered. That simply wouldn't do.

His mind whirling, Darryl plonked down in the chair next to Velma and reached for her hand. He had to come up with a plan that would keep her safe. And he had to do it quickly.

The two sat in silence, their hands entwined. He saw the look Maggie gave him. At first he thought it was one of displeasure, but soon realized it was the complete opposite. Without warning, she left the room. Leaving them alone.

"Velma," he said softly. "Did you hear what I said earlier?"

She raised her eyebrows. "The part when you said *I love you*? I heard."

Her words were like a sucker punch to the stomach. She left him hanging, not saying where she stood on the matter. He guessed her lack of emotion said it all.

"Your bath is ready," Maggie said as she returned to the sitting room. "You'll find towels in there, and everything else you need."

Darryl reluctantly let her hand go. He stood when Velma did, then sat down again the moment she was gone. "What are you doing?" Maggie hissed when Velma had left the room. "She is confused enough without you adding to her problems."

Maggie was right. Except he didn't want to desert Velma. Nor did he intend to leave her without protection. He was ahead with his work, which meant he could stay here for a few days. Couldn't he? "What if I said I'm in love with her?" He studied Maggie as she was studying him.

"Is that even possible?" she asked. "I mean, you haven't known each other that long. Heck, she can't remember her life before you rescued her." The expression on her face changed. It was almost a grimace. "Now the outlaw knows she's here in town, Velma is in grave danger, isn't she?"

He didn't want to say it out loud, but Darryl knew he had to tell the truth. "Her life has been in danger since the moment she was taken hostage at the bank." The thought of it had Darryl feeling hollow. His heart felt as though it was twisting. Without the proper protection, Velma would not survive. He shook his head briefly, then stared at Maggie. "I can't lose her, Maggie. I just can't."

Maggie stared at him intently. "How much do you love Velma? Enough to marry her?"

Without a word, Darryl sat and pondered the questions. Did he love her that much? He didn't have to think long. Before she arrived, he was simply going through the motions. When he saw her being dragged and threatened by Butch Carpenter, it crushed his heart. "I do love her that much,"

Darryl said. "But whether she'll agree is another thing altogether."

~*~

Darryl was sipping coffee when Velma returned. She looked far more relaxed now, compared to the way she was earlier. Not that he could blame her. Velma had been through an horrific trauma. When that smoke covered her, Darryl didn't know what to think. Butch Carpenter had her in a position where he could have killed her there and then. The sheriff's gun to the man's head was probably the only thing that saved her.

"You look refreshed," he said as he put the mug of coffee on the side table.

"I feel better," she answered. "Much better."

He tapped the chair next to him, indicating for Velma to sit, which she did. "I know this may come as a surprise, but I need to ask you something," Darryl said, staring out of the window. It was important Velma was not in danger from outside.

When he turned around, she had tilted her head sideways, and studied him. "Go ahead and ask," she said warily.

Darryl dropped to the floor, one knee bent. "Velma, will you marry me? It will help to keep you safe, since you'll be with me." Once the words were out, he held his breath waiting for her answer.

"Are you serious?" Velma growled. "I won't marry you to keep safe." She stood and stormed past him.

When he glanced up, Maggie was watching from the doorway. "I wouldn't have accepted either," she said gently. "You made it sound like the only reason you wanted to marry Velma was to protect her." She raised her eyebrows as if questioning his sanity.

Darryl slapped a hand to his forehead. "I messed up, didn't I?"

"You most certainly did," Maggie scolded. "Why didn't you say you loved her? Protection doesn't even come into it. Only love matters to women."

"What should I do now?" Darryl asked, disgusted with himself. "How can I fix this?" His heart was breaking, but this time it was due to his own stupidity.

"Go home, clean up, and come back in time to eat."

If that was all it took, Darryl would be ecstatic. Unfortunately, he didn't believe Velma would make it so easy for him.

Chapter Seventeen

Velma had enjoyed the hot bath. It had calmed her down. A lot. As she'd slid down into the inviting bath, full of bubbles, it held the promise of comfort. Now, though, she was more than a little angry at Darryl. She had every right to be. Didn't she? His words had reversed the comfort and calmness the hot bath had supplied.

If he loved her, it would be different. Except he didn't. Had she dreamed he'd told her he loved her? While he carried her to the doctor's office. She shook herself mentally. Surely if he truly loved her, he would have said so. Velma couldn't believe what was happening.

Despite losing her memory, she still knew she had feelings for Darryl. But for his part, Darryl only wanted to protect her. After that, then what? He would be lumbered with a wife he had no interest in.

Or even worse, he would be injured or killed trying to keep her alive. Velma knew she couldn't live with herself if Darryl were to die in the process of saving her. She was more confused than ever.

Because of his dreadful proposal, her thoughts were running away with her. There were far too many unanswered questions. Decisions to be made that she couldn't make. Not because she didn't want to, but because she didn't know enough about her life before Hopetoun. Before she arrived here.

And Darryl saved her.

Never would Velma forget what Darryl had done for her. If not for him, she would be dead. Buried in the small grave yard on the outskirts of town. In an unmarked grave. With no one to visit or care.

A sob left her lips.

Darryl had done a lot for her. Far more than could be expected. This was the one thing she could do for him. Velma could not marry him and put Darryl's life in danger. One day he would thank her for it.

She cried all the tears she could muster while no one was there to see them. Her heart broke for what she had to do, and that was keep her distance. Darryl would be better off because of it.

She would be doing him a favor.

He could go back to his wagon making, and his cottage, and forget she ever existed. The moment the outlaw was caught, Velma could go back to her former life. Take up where she left off. Darryl would soon forget her when she was no longer around.

The older woman knew what Velma needed. It was as though Maggie had known her all her life. She only hoped Maggie hadn't scolded Darryl too much. Of course, she would have – the moment Velma was out of earshot. She knew Maggie well.

Did that mean Darryl had left? Gone forever? She would find out soon enough. As she sat at the window in her room, feeling sorry for herself, a thought struck Velma like an arrow to the heart.

What if the outlaw killed Darryl on his way home? Plucking him off his horse and ensuring he was dead? It was feasible he was still around. He was determined to eliminate Velma for what she'd witnessed.

Despite the fact she barely remembered that day. She couldn't even remember who she was, for goodness sake.

She strode into the sitting room with a mind to tell Darryl to leave. To never see her again. Except he wasn't there, and her heart shattered. Even though that's what she wanted. Deep down, Velma knew it wasn't true. What she really wanted was Darryl, but she needed him to stay safe. How could that happen if he was protecting her?

At least now he was gone, and wouldn't be back. So why did she feel so hollow knowing she'd never see him again?

Velma was all cried out, otherwise she would have sat herself down and had a good cry. Wasn't she the one who wanted him gone? So why did knowing he left hurt so much? Maggie was in the kitchen cooking, as she often was. It seemed to be where she was the happiest. Velma felt deep down she knew how to cook, but her memory wasn't allowing her to remember much at all. Not the good things anyway.

As she closed her eyes each night, the vision of the bank robbery was vivid. Bullets flying, hitting the teller. She was the lucky one – if you could call it that. Had she been shot and then put in that horrid box, she would not have survived. Velma knew that to be true. Darryl would have found her dead, laying in a pool of her own blood.

She shivered at the thought.

Wandering over to the window, Velma glanced at her surroundings. It seemed peaceful enough. Townsfolk were wandering about, despite the snow and the cold. Only a few more days, and it would be Christmas, Maggie told her. There must be something she could do to prepare for the special day.

It was then Velma remembered Darryl was invited to join them. Would he still come, or stay away because of her? It seemed like her heart twisted every time she thought of her rescuer. As much as she wanted to deny them, her feelings for Darryl refused to dissipate.

Spinning around at the sound of heavy pans dropping in the kitchen, Velma went to ensure Maggie was alright. Standing in the doorway, her heart pounding, Velma bent down and helped pick up the errant pans.

"Thank you," Maggie told her. "I tried to carry too many at once. How are you feeling after your hot bath?"

"A lot better," Velma said, and although her inner thoughts were unhelpful, she still felt better than before.

As she stood up, Velma felt the hair on her arms and the back of her neck stand up. Her heart rate accelerated, and she was certain danger was close by.

Velma spun around to face her would-be killer.

Chapter Eighteen

Darryl stood in the doorway taking in the scene before him. The two wonderful women before him had become more like family than anything else. "You really need to keep the door locked," he said, before noticing the terror on Velma's face. Did she think he was Butch Carpenter? His heart twisted. The last thing he wanted to do was frighten her. "I'm sorry," he said gently. "I didn't mean to scare you. Either of you."

He stepped forward and held Velma in his arms. She was shaking. He'd done that to her. He hadn't thought about the consequences of his actions. The fact he was a frequent visitor to the boarding house these days, made him feel safe in his assumption he was expected. Now he realized Maggie may have kept it a surprise.

Glancing up at the two, Maggie scowled. "You're right, of course. I should keep the front door locked. I never have. It's always been safe here."

"Until I turned up," Velma said quietly.

Darryl pushed her away, but only a little. He wanted to look into her face when he said the words. "None of this is your fault. You are an innocent victim in all this." It was true, but getting that message through to Velma could be difficult.

Nonetheless, she nodded. Did that mean she understood or was simply trying to pacify him? "I thought you weren't coming back. Ever," Velma whispered.

Her words confused him. "Why would you think that? Maggie invited me to supper." He glanced across at Maggie. She shook her head as if to say she had no idea why Velma would think that way.

"No matter," Maggie finally said. "Supper will be ready soon. Why don't you two rest up in the sitting room. I'll call you when the food is ready."

Darryl's arms were still around Velma, although she wasn't as close to him as he would like. She glanced up at him and raised her eyebrows. A silent message to tell him she couldn't go anywhere. Reluctantly, Darryl dropped his arms, and waved Velma ahead of him.

She sat down almost the moment they arrived in the sitting room. Darryl stoked the fire and added more fuel, as it was burning low. He then turned to face Velma. "About earlier," he said, brushing ashes from his hands. "The words didn't come out right." Velma frowned. "I mean…"

What did he mean? Darryl took a long fortifying breath, then started over. "Velma, I have come to love you. I know we haven't known each other long, but I've never felt like this before." He dropped to one knee, again, and continued. "When I saw that man with his hands on you, and a gun pointed at you, it made me realize how much I really love you. I already loved you, but that made me understand I couldn't lose you." He stopped then. Darryl knew he was babbling. He couldn't help himself.

"What are you trying to say?" Velma asked, trying to hold back her smile.

"Velma, will you marry me?" Darryl asked, gazing into her face. He reached into his pocket and pulled out a small velvet box. "If the size isn't right, it can be adjusted."

Velma gasped. Was it because she didn't want to marry him? His heart thudded. She was going to say no. He knew she was. Seconds seemed to turn to minutes, and minutes to hours, as he waited for her to answer.

He flipped open the lid to the box, showing her the beautiful engagement ring he'd purchased at the mercantile on his way here. Her silence was killing him. It was clear Velma didn't want too marry him. He was about to flip the lid closed again when she answered. But not in words.

Velma reached into the box and slipped it on her finger. She gazed at it from every possible angle. Was that a yes? His heart felt like it was about to explode.

Finally her eyes returned to Darryl. A sly smile crossed her lips. "I would be very pleased to marry you," she said, then pulled Darryl to his feet. For the first time, he brushed her lips with his own, his arms wrapped around her. He had joy in his heart, but knew the hard work of keeping his fiancée safe had only just begun.

Darryl drank down the last of his coffee, and thanked Maggie for the meal. He also thanked the two women for the good company. Then he stood and stretched his legs.

"You be careful on the trip home," Maggie said. "You need to be especially careful since it's almost dark."

Darryl stared at her, confused. "I'm not going anywhere," he said. "My horse is at the livery, and being well looked after. I'm in a cozy and warm place, and this is where I'm staying."

"But…" Velma began, and Darryl threw her a look. He was more determined than ever to stay and protect both women. "Tomorrow we go and see the preacher," he said. "Once we're married you can come home with me." He thought about that for a moment. "Maggie, perhaps you should come, too. I don't want you to be in danger, either."

Maggie shook her head, as he knew she would. The woman was as stubborn as they come. "I'll get some bedding for you," she said, then hurried off to do just that. Not that he would be cold here in the sitting room. It was warm and cozy. Darryl just hoped he didn't drift off to sleep when he was meant to be looking out for the two women.

It wasn't long before Maggie returned, her arms full of blankets and a pillow. Darryl kicked off his boots, and pulled off his gun belt, keeping the gun with him. He hoped and prayed Butch Carpenter wouldn't come calling during the night. Trouble was, you never knew with someone like him.

"Well, goodnight, then," Maggie said, and headed to bed.

Velma stood, and yawned. "I'll be off, too," she said.

Darryl pulled her in for a hug. "I like this engaged stuff," he said with a chuckle. "I couldn't do this when we were only friends." He held her tight, then kissed Velma gently on the lips. When she leaned back, Velma put her fingers to her lips, and smiled.

Darryl hoped her lips were tingling, just as his were.

~*~

All was quiet, and the women had gone to bed some time ago. Darryl had snoozed here and there, but knew he needed to keep his wits about him. Maggie's sofa wasn't the most comfortable to sleep on, especially given his height. Still, the discomfort was worth it to save these wonderful ladies.

Darryl sat on the side of the sofa, checked the fire and added more fuel to it, then wandered over to the window. Apart from the occasional drunk, it seemed quiet enough outside. He strode to the front door for at least the sixth time that night, and ensured it was locked. As he suspected, it was.

He went to the back door for the same reason. It was locked, too, as he was certain it would be. Darryl went to each of the women's rooms, and stood outside, ensuring all was well. At least, he did the best he could from outside their rooms.

He should have known Butch Carpenter would not show himself so soon. He would wait until it was least expected, then attack. Like he had at the railway station earlier in the day. Only this time, Darryl would be right there, beside Velma. He would be with her every step of the way. He was proficient with firearms, but Darryl was certain Butch Carpenter would be, too.

Heading back to the sitting room, he heard a sound. One that shouldn't be there. He hurried to the front door, since that's where the sound seemed to be coming from. He moved quietly, but swiftly. As he suspected, someone on the other side was rattling the door handle. Darryl went to the window, and peeked out, trying not to show himself.

He breathed a sigh of relief when he saw Sheriff Dodd standing there. Darryl opened the door to him. "I didn't expect to see you here tonight," Darryl told the sheriff as he ushered him inside.

The sheriff shook the excess snow off his hat and coat before making himself comfortable in one of the chairs close to the fire. "It's freezing out there," he said, holding his hands toward the fire.

"I am not surprised," Darryl said. "Let me get you a coffee. That will warm you up."

Sheriff Dodd did not refuse the offer. "No sign of Butch Carpenter?" Darryl asked. Stupidly, he realized afterwards. If there was, the sheriff would have dealt with him.

"In one way I wish there was," Peter Dodd said. "In another, I hope he's left town and is gone for good."

"Except, that being the case, Velma would be looking over her shoulder for the rest of her life," Darryl said. "And that will never do. She needs closure. Needs to know he will never bother her again."

Sheriff Dodd stared at him for long moments. "Of course, you're right," he said. A short time later

Darryl handed him a mug of coffee, and sat down with his own coffee. "Maggie made it extra strong."

"She's a good woman, is Maggie," Sheriff Dodd said, and Darryl wondered if there was anything between the two of them. They seemed very familiar with each other. But then again, he was like that with Maggie, too. The truth was, Maggie was a friend to everyone.

As they sat talking, the front door handle rattled. Sheriff Dodd put a finger to his lips, then went to the same window Darryl had a short time earlier. He pulled back the curtain the least he could do and still see who was standing there.

Even with the moonlight, it was too dark to tell. If he had to guess, Darryl would say it was Butch Carpenter. It surprised him, because he didn't pick the man as a risk taker. And yet, he'd tried to kill Velma in daylight, on the busy train platform, with passengers and porters all around him. The man had no fear.

"He's on the run," Sheriff Dodd said solemnly. He pulled open the front door, but the outlaw was nowhere to be seen.

Darryl knew this was just the beginning. No matter where she was, Butch Carpenter would find her.

Chapter Nineteen

Velma was dazed. Half asleep and barely awake. She pulled the thick robe around herself, and staggered out into the sitting room. That appeared to be where the sounds were coming from. Except that wasn't the direction the other sounds were. They were closer.

"Velma," Darryl said, surprise in his voice. "What are you doing up? Couldn't you sleep?"

She shook her head. "It was the tapping. In my room," Velma said, rubbing at her eyes hoping that would make everything clearer. It didn't.

Before she could say another word, Sheriff Dodd ran toward her room. She hadn't noticed the sheriff until that moment. Her eyes had focused only on Darryl. "What's going on?" she demanded, but instead of answering, Darryl pulled her close against her.

"He's here. Trying to locate you." She gasped, and Darryl pushed her back a little to look into her face. "It's all conjecture. He doesn't know where you are, I'm certain."

Velma wasn't so sure. "That was him tapping at the window? He knows I'm here," she said. Velma could hear the panic in her own voice, and had no doubt Darryl could as well. "What…what about Maggie? Is she in danger because of me?" She wouldn't cry. No she wouldn't. Even though she'd put her best friend in the world in danger. "You should have let him kill me. That way no one else would be at risk." Her voice wavered, and her tears fell, despite her best efforts. This was no longer about saving herself. It was about keeping her friends out of a dangerous situation.

Sheriff Dodd returned. "There's no one there now, but that doesn't mean he wasn't there before. I'm going outside. I need to finish this." The sheriff ran a hand through his hair, making it a mess. He glanced about, stopping when he located his hat and coat.

"It's not safe to go alone," Darryl implored him. "Besides, it's pitch black and you won't find him with only the moonlight to guide you."

Darryl was right, and Velma knew it. The sheriff seemed torn. He wanted to chase down her pursuer, knowing he was nearby, except it could mean his death. "Please don't," she pleaded. "I couldn't live with myself if he killed you. Either of you." Velma held back a sob. She desperately wanted to return to her room, and let her emotions take over, but it was too dangerous. Butch Carpenter could easily smash the glass window, reach inside and shoot her.

Her heart pounded so badly she felt light headed. Velma sat down on one of the chairs. At least here she could see what the two men were up to, and know they were safe. "Did you get any sleep?" she asked Darryl.

He studied her. Was he deciding whether to tell the truth or humor her? "A little. Enough," he said abruptly. "Don't you go worrying about me. You are the one we need to worry about."

"And Maggie," she whispered, as though she dare not think what may happen if that evil man got into Maggie's room.

Sheriff Dodd's head shot up. Then he was running toward Maggie's bedroom. Velma heard him tapping on the door, and calling Maggie's name. After that everything was a blur. Amidst the chaos that followed, Velma didn't think she would ever be the same again.

Darryl pushed her behind him, and held tight to his gun. "Don't move," he said. Velma knew he was trying to protect her, but she didn't want him to die in the process.

The gunshot they heard put them both on alert. Right now, it was anyone's guess who shot who. Was Maggie alright? And what about the sheriff?

Velma could do nothing. Darryl had made sure of that.

In what seemed like hours, but was only minutes, both Sheriff Dodd and Maggie entered the sitting room. Velma ran to her friend. The two women held each other tight. "I'm so sorry, Maggie," Velma whispered. "This is all my fault." This time she let her emotions rule her head.

"Nothing to apologize for," Maggie told her. "I'm fine, Peter, er, the sheriff is fine."

Velma was confused. "We heard a gunshot." She stared at her friend, trying to understand the situation.

"Sheriff Dodd took a shot at the man."

"He was hit, but I only grazed him," the sheriff said. "He moved quickly. If I hadn't got in there so quickly, Maggie would have…" He stopped talking, and Maggie ran to him. The sheriff held her close. They seemed comfortable in each other's arms.

Maggie and the sheriff. No wonder Sheriff Dodd took off so quickly. How they'd managed to keep it a secret all this time, Velma had no idea.

Velma suddenly felt a chill. She glanced at the fire, it was still burning, but almost out. She threw some logs on the fire, then stood. As she turned back, the silhouette of a man stood at the window. Her voice died. Instead she pointed to the window. Darryl lifted his gun, and didn't hesitate.

~*~

The explosion of noise rang through Velma's ears. Her entire body trembled, but her head, it was like a hundred church bells ringing at the same time, and she was standing in the midst of it all.

Shattered glass covered much of the sitting room, and a shiver raced down her spine. Despite Velma standing close to the fire. Darryl's arm was around her, and she welcomed the comfort he gave.

Did this mean her ordeal was over? She could only hope.

When she glanced across, Sheriff Dodd held his gun in an upright position, ready to fire. It begged the question, which of the two men actually shot Butch Carpenter?

"You stay here with the ladies," Sheriff Dodd told Darryl. "I'll check if he's still alive."

Velma wasn't sure it was safe, but at least now, it was close to sunrise, and no longer pitch black outside.

Despite what the sheriff said, Darryl was on his heels. "Stay here," he demanded of both the women. They huddled together once more.

It seemed like forever before the two men returned. Both their faces grim. "He's gone. Two bullets to the chest," Sheriff Dodd said sadly. "I would have preferred a trial, but he left us no choice."

Darryl pulled Velma into his arms. "It's over. You're safe now."

She might be safe, but would that mean Darryl no longer wanted to marry her?

Chapter Twenty

Darryl was shocked to hear both he and the sheriff had shot the attacker. As Sheriff Dodd had said, it was a shame there would be no trial, and therefore no punishment, but they were left with no choice.

He now knew Butch Carpenter had broken into Maggie's room via the window and was halfway across the room when the sheriff forced his way into the room. It was the very moment the criminal lifted his gun and pointed it at the sheriff. He then pivoted and pointed it toward Maggie. That was the moment the sheriff shot the man, except he was already on the move.

Grazing him was not enough to slow the would-be murderer down. He fled the same way he came in, despite being shot in the shoulder. As evidenced minutes ago, it wasn't enough to put him off or to kill him.

As he held Velma in his arms, Darryl knew he would do it all over again. He'd never killed another person before, and hoped he never needed to again. In this case, he knew both he and the sheriff were justified. When they'd gone outside, Butch

Carpenter held a gun in each hand. It could have been a massacre if they'd not eliminated him as quickly as they had.

"I'll contact the marshals the moment the telegraph office opens," Sheriff Dodd said, breaking into Darryl's thoughts. "In the meantime, I will arrange for him to be taken to the morgue." He leaned down and kissed Maggie on the lips. "I'll be back as soon as I can, my love," he whispered, but not quiet enough the others couldn't hear.

"Maggie, do you have a spare towel I can use?" Darryl's request had her frowning, but Maggie left the room and returned with a thick towel. Taking it, he explained. "I don't want you ladies witnessing the devastation outside the window." It was the least he could do. It was bad enough Darryl and the sheriff had to endure it. Ladies were far more delicate, as far as he could tell.

"That's very thoughtful of you, Darryl," Maggie said. "Time for coffee, I believe." She hurried into the kitchen, leaving him alone with Velma who seemed somewhat withdrawn.

"Is everything alright?" he asked, lifting her face to him. "I know it's a lot to take in, but the danger is over now." He kissed her on the cheek, and pulled her close. Velma gasped.

Glancing down, he discovered the sadness covering her face. The reason for it eluded him. Velma stepped back from him, and played with the ring on her finger. Finally she pulled it off and handed it back to him. He saw the tears that swam in her eyes, but she fought them back. "What is this?" he asked, staring down at the ring he'd given her only yesterday.

Velma licked her lips. "You don't need to marry me now. The threat is over."

Darryl couldn't have been more shocked at her words. "It was never about protecting you. I fumbled my words that first time, I know, and that's on me." Darryl held the ring between his fingers, then reached for her hand. "Velma, I love you with all my heart. Will you marry me?" he asked as he slipped the ring back on her finger.

"I love you, too," Velma whispered, then buried her face against his chest.

It was at that moment Maggie strolled in carrying a tray of steaming hot drinks and sliced cake. "I'm sorry," she said, and turned to leave the room.

"Don't go," Darryl said. "You are the first to know. Velma and I are getting married." He couldn't help the sly smile that came to his lips.

"But you…" Maggie shook her head. "I give up!" she said, then indicated for them to sit down. Sheriff Dodd arrived back moments later, and was relieved to find coffee was being offered.

"He is now at the undertaker's," the sheriff said. "I know the marshals will be happy with this outcome. The man has wreaked havoc everywhere he's been."

Darryl was relieved the sheriff didn't announce the man was a murderer many times over. Bank robber and hired gun. He surely didn't expect to live very long.

They all sat and sipped their drinks and ate cake. It was a little after sunrise. Darryl couldn't get over the irony of it all. First they were terrorized by a killer, then he and the sheriff killed the man, and now they all celebrated by eating cake.

Well, not celebrating exactly. This was Maggie doing what she does best. Making everyone feel comfortable and at home.

No one mentioned how strange this entire scenario was. They all drank and ate as though it was something they did on a regular basis.

"I'll make breakfast soon," Maggie said to no one in particular. "Bacon and eggs on toast? How does that sound?"

Sheriff Dodd reached over and patted her hand. "Maggie, you don't have to do that," he said gently. Darryl was beginning to wonder if Maggie was in shock. It was highly likely she was, and perhaps even Velma. It all seemed rather surreal to him.

"Should I fetch the doc?" Darryl asked gently. He didn't want either of the women to suffer unnecessarily.

Peter Dodd nodded his head. "It would be a good idea, I think."

Darryl leaned into Velma, and kissed her cheek. "I'll be back shortly. Don't go anywhere." He pulled on his thick coat and headed out the door. As he did so, he glanced down where Butch Carpenter had previously laid. There was blood everywhere. He made a mental note to clean it up when he returned.

He then headed to the doctor's office, hoping he didn't wake the man.

Doctor Gabe Spencer snapped his medical bag closed. "They're both in shock, but that's to be expected. Nothing much to be done," he said. "Except for rest. What about you two? You're probably the same."

Sheriff Dodd shrugged the suggestion away. "Not a first for me," he said firmly.

"Except this time you were protecting your lady." So it wasn't as big a secret as Darryl thought it might be. "I'll check you both out while I'm here. No harm in doing so." When he finished examining the men, he headed for the front door. "Same for you two. Rest up. Take it easy for a day or two." Doc Spencer was gone before they could protest.

"You heard the doc," Maggie said. "I hereby declare today a day of rest and thankfulness."

Darryl couldn't disagree with that.

Despite the difficult time behind them all, the four friends celebrated Christmas at the boarding house two days later. Maggie and Velma put together a wonderful spread, which included a turkey with all the trimmings, and a variety of roasted vegetables. There was Christmas pudding and various cakes and slices Maggie had been preparing for a number of days.

She was determined the dead killer was not going to spoil Christmas day for them. The others agreed. It was Darryl's first Christmas with Velma, and it definitely wouldn't be their last. He wanted to ensure it was special for her.

This was the happiest Darryl had felt on Christmas day for many years. He wasn't being pressured into a marriage he didn't want, but was comfortable in the fact his soon-to-be wife sat closely beside him, but more importantly, was safe.

~*~

After speaking with the preacher a few days later, a wedding date was decided. Finally that day arrived.

The entire town attended, with the businesses shutting their doors for the celebration. Everyone wanted to attend the wedding of the two most eligible bachelors in town, not to mention their much-loved Maggie. Most of the townsfolk didn't know Velma, but knew if Darryl chose her to be his wife, she was special.

Both Darryl and Peter Dodd stood at the front of the church wearing their Sunday best. They looked back at their beautiful brides, who stood waiting for the organist to begin playing. Gabe Spencer had a bride on each arm, and couldn't appear more proud if he tried.

A special friendship had resulted from the danger these four had faced together. Darryl was certain they would remain friends as long as they lived.

A shiver went through him as the music began. He exchanged a glance with Peter Dodd, then they looked to their brides. This was the happiest day of Darryl's life, and he was certain it was the same for Peter.

The entire church was packed. Everyone stood as the brides began their march down the aisle. Hands reached out to the brides, sending their good wishes.

This was a day Darryl knew he would never forget. He hoped it was the same for Velma, and of course Peter and Maggie. They were all so happy to have been able to share the day.

Standing on the steps of the church after the ceremony, everyone cheered them on. Rice was thrown at each couple, and according to Maggie, it was said to be a symbol of fertility and prosperity. If that was true, they would all have a large dose of each.

They'd planned to leave the church, then move to the diner for a celebratory luncheon together. A quiet affair with only the four of them.

Except it didn't turn out that way. In an unexpected turn of events, the townsfolk had arranged a celebration in the church hall. They were directed there, and Darryl stood at the door to the hall staring in amazement.

Before him stood table after table of food – all supplied by those who lived in Hopetoun. Darryl had always been a loner, and hadn't mingled a lot. He didn't attend the dances, and only occasionally went to church.

He glanced across at his new bride. She appeared as shocked as he was. Peter and Maggie didn't appear quite so surprised.

There was a table set aside for the two couples to enable them to sit down as they ate. The center of the room was empty. To allow dancing, Darryl guessed. When the music began, he knew he was right. Suddenly it stopped again.

"Quiet down, everyone," someone shouted. "It's time for the two happy couples to have their first dance together as husband and wife." This was not something he expected. How many years had it been since he'd danced? He didn't know, but Darryl did know it was far too many.

Regardless, the two grooms took their new wives by the hand and led them out to the dance floor. No matter how bad a dancer he was, Darryl was determined to make the day memorable for Velma. When they were in position, the music began again. It was slow, and allowed Darryl to get his bearings. Only he knew he would embarrass himself. Not to mention his new bride.

"Put your arms around me, and simply sway in time with the music," Velma whispered.

Darryl did exactly that, and he couldn't have been happier. Before they were married, he would not have been allowed to dance this close to Velma. His heart fluttered when he thought about the love they shared.

 Epilogue

Three years later…

Velma knew it was past time Darryl had a break. He was busy on his latest wagon project, which was due a week after Christmas. She reached for the broom Darryl kept outside, and cleared the path to his workshop.

She needed to open the heavy door, but it was too much for her, especially with her hands full. "Darryl," Velma called as she banged on the door. It wasn't long before she heard footsteps.

The door slowly opened, and he ushered her inside. "What are you doing out here in the cold? You don't even have a shawl on, let alone a coat." He appeared annoyed, but Velma knew he was only looking out for her.

"Henry is having a nap," she said. "So I decided to bring you a coffee and something to eat." She handed over the drink and snacks she'd brought for him.

"It's good, thank you," Darryl said, then took another bite of cake.

"You need to finish up soon," Velma told him. "Peter and Maggie will be here shortly. To plan for Christmas day."

The expression on her husband's face told Velma all she needed to know – he had completely forgotten they were coming to visit. "Sorry, Sweetheart," he said, leaning in and kissing her cheek. I got so wrapped up in what I was doing, I completely forgot."

Velma wasn't surprised. Darryl's work was very important to him, not to mention his customers who came from miles away to have one of his custom made wagons. Besides, she couldn't complain. People paid a premium price to have a Darryl Franklin original.

"I better get back," Velma said. "Henry will be awake soon." The thought of their two-year-old son had warmth flooding through her veins. Velma patted her stomach – it wouldn't be long before their next precious cargo would show his or herself. She privately wished for a girl, but as long as their baby was happy and healthy, Velma didn't mind.

Darryl opened the heavy door for her, and stood watching Velma to ensure she got back to their home safely. Before he closed it again, their visitors arrived.

Maggie held their two-year-old son, Jacob on her lap. It was a sight to behold. The four friends had become even more close as the years had rolled on. Peter Dodd parked the buggy, and took young Jacob from her. He passed the boy over to Darryl, then helped his pregnant wife to the ground.

Their sons had grown up together, and were only weeks apart. Velma couldn't wait to see how close their subsequent babies were, and hoped they became close friends like the boys.

To think, this friendship came from what could have been an absolute tragedy. Instead, they'd all become lifelong friends.

"Oooh," she said, then reached for Darryl's hand.

He glanced up and smiled. "That's my daughter," he said. Velma knew no matter what, Darryl would love this baby unconditionally, as he did her and little Henry.

From the Author

Thank you so much for reading my book – I hope you enjoyed it.

I would greatly appreciate you leaving a review where you purchased, even if it is only a one-liner. It helps to have my books more visible!

About the Author

Multi-published, award-winning and bestselling author Cheryl Wright, former secretary, debt collector, account manager, writing coach, and shopping tour hostess, loves reading.

She writes historical romantic suspense and historical western romance.

She lives in Melbourne, Australia, and is married with two adult children and has six grandchildren, and twin great-grandchildren.

When she's not writing, she can be found in her craft room making greeting cards.

$\mathcal{L}inks$

Website: *http://www.cheryl-wright.com/*

Facebook Reader Group:
https://www.facebook.com/groups/cherylwrightauthor/

Join My Newsletter:

https://cheryl-wright.com/newsletter/
(and receive a free book)

www.ingramcontent.com/pod-product-compliance
Lightning Source LLC
Chambersburg PA
CBHW070404200726
48294CB00003B/1072